108

THE COURAGE
OF ANNA CAMERON

Nurse Anna Cameron had been sent to prison for six months for neglecting a patient in her care — the old lady had died because she had not been given her prescribed medication. Anna knew that the fault really lay with Sharon, the young nurse who had been helping her. On her release, Anna finds that all this trouble has placed a great strain on her three children — and on her marriage. Somehow, she must find the courage to pick up the pieces of her shattered life . . .

Books by Jane Carrick
in the Linford Romance Library:

DIAMONDS ON THE LAKE
A PEARL FOR LOVE
A HANDFUL OF MIST

JANE CARRICK

THE COURAGE
OF
ANNA CAMERON

Complete and Unabridged

LINFORD
Leicester

First published in Great Britain in 1985

First Linford Edition
published 2003

British Library CIP Data

Carrick, Jane
  The courage of Anna Cameron.—
  Large print ed.—
  Linford romance library
  1. Love stories
  2. Large type books
  I. Title
  823.9'14 [F]

  ISBN 0–7089–9471–7

Published by
F. A. Thorpe (Publishing)
Anstey, Leicestershire

Set by Words & Graphics Ltd.
Anstey, Leicestershire
Printed and bound in Great Britain by
T. J. International Ltd., Padstow, Cornwall

This book is printed on acid-free paper

Deeply Hurt

The old Victorian mansion house had never looked more beautiful. In the neat flower beds, stately tulips towered high above the fragrant softness of wallflowers, whilst two gardeners ensured that no weeds marred the well-kept lawns and that the edges were trimmed to perfection.

Over the past six months, Hugh Cameron had seen the place in all weathers, and now, on this his last visit, it seemed appropriate that the sun shone with the pale warmth of spring. Perhaps it was an omen for the future, he thought, as he followed the signs which took him to the administration office, then parked in front of the wide entrance.

This was a new block, recently built, and Hugh's eyes turned towards the swing doors. He had timed his arrival for exactly two o'clock, and as he checked the clock on the dashboard of the car, the doors suddenly flew open and his wife appeared, her old brown suitcase clasped in her hand.

How pale and thin she looked, thought Hugh. Only eight months ago they had celebrated their twenty-eighth wedding anniversary, and he had a sudden mental picture of Anna as she had looked that evening, in her elegant green velvet gown and wearing the single rope of pearls he had given her.

Something caught at Hugh's heart as he saw the lost, almost sightless look on her face, and he leapt from the car, striding forward to meet her, taking her case and kissing her cheek.

'I — I'm in good time,' he said awkwardly. 'Are you OK, Anna? Ready to go now?'

She nodded wordlessly as he settled her into the passenger seat, then stowed her case in the boot. The car wheels crunched as he once again drove along the winding driveway.

Hugh stopped the car before driving into the main road, and for a brief moment Anna looked at the large notice displayed near the gate — H.M. Prison, Poplar Lodge.

She held her breath as Hugh turned the car into the open road, then released it with a tiny sigh. She was free!

★   ★   ★

'Would you like to stop somewhere for a cup of tea, darling?' Hugh asked uncomfortably, aware of the deep tension within her and the lack of ease between them.

Ought he to behave normally with her, and try to pretend that everything was just as it had been, or would she prefer to speak openly about her prison sentence and the nightmare six months she had spent away from her family?

'I'll wait till I get home,' she decided. 'We can have a cup of tea then. I had my lunch before I was — discharged.'

3

'Oh, that's good.'

The gently rolling fields and faint blue hills were familiar to her. They had often driven along this road between Edinburgh and Castleden, the small town where she and Hugh had lived all their married life.

Now Anna fought down the hard lump in her throat.

'How are the children?' she asked huskily.

'Fine,' Hugh told her quickly — too quickly, she thought. 'They're all well. Peter is working hard at his new job with Coronet Insurance, and Jill is still struggling through her biology — as well as her other lessons. Myra's busy with the children, of course . . . Wendy has started school and Paul goes to nursery school now that he's turned three. Charles, of course, is still climbing the ladder at Foster & Davis.'

He pulled himself up short as he mentioned his son-in-law's firm. How easy it was to remind Anna about her experience. The very name of Foster must be an anathema to her, but her voice didn't tremble as she asked about her grandchildren.

'I can't wait to see my wee Wendy again, and Paul, of course. Is she as full of mischief as ever? She used to be into everything. Boys are supposed to be more boisterous, but Wendy was always worse than Paul. He has been such a dear, quiet little boy.'

'He's not so quiet now,' Hugh said, 'and Myra has arranged dancing lessons for Wendy. She's determined to have Paul up on a horse, too, as soon as he is old enough. You know what Myra is like with show jumping!'

Anna's eyes dulled a little. Her elder daughter had always wanted more than they had been able to provide for her. She had wanted her own horse, as well as ballet lessons and long holidays in France to improve her knowledge of the language.

Myra was no doubt determined to give Wendy and Paul the advantages she never had herself. There had never been enough money . . .

'How's the business, Hugh?' she asked anxiously.

'OK. Nothing to worry about,' he assured her, but this time she knew by his tone that he was lying.

Anna sighed. Perhaps now that she was home she could help him a little. But how? After all, she'd been jailed for causing the death of an old lady by her neglect. How could she ever hope to revive a builder's business?

They had reached Castleden now and Anna looked about her eagerly as Hugh drove down the main street. Then remembrance crowded in upon her and she shrank back in her seat. Would her friends still want to see her?

They were past the centre of the town now and approaching their nice, settled housing estate built shortly after the war. Their own house was third on the right, a pretty house with two matching bay windows and a built-in garage. A path beside the house led to

Hugh's builder's yard, situated on a parallel road.

He was soon opening the door with his key, then Anna was in the tiny hall and hurrying into the living room. She had expected the family to be gathered there, and to leap up to meet her in order to surprise her, as they had so often done in the past. But the room was empty and Anna couldn't stem the feeling of disappointment.

She stood in the middle of the living-room whilst Hugh busied himself in the hall. How small it all looked, and how shabby!

For a moment, Anna's housewifely instincts were up in arms, then she sank gratefully into her old favourite chair by the fireside. The room was in shade so that, despite the sunshine, it felt cold and unwelcoming, but Hugh quickly switched on the fire.

'I — I had thought the children might be here,' Anna began, a little tremulously.

'Peter's at work and Jill's at college. I

expect Myra will be along later. Sit back, dear, I'll make you a cup of tea.'

Anna listened to the kindness in her husband's voice, though she could see the awkwardness in him.

The clock on the mantelpiece chimed three o'clock and Anna stared at it, remembering how long it had taken her and Hugh to save up for its purchase.

Her husband suddenly appeared with a small tray of tea and buscuits. There was only one cup.

'Aren't you having tea?' she asked.

'No, I've just noticed the time. I have to see the bank manager in a quarter of an hour. It's an appointment I must keep, Anna.'

'Then . . . then you need money, Hugh?' Anna wanted to know.

'Nothing for you to worry about,' he said heartily. 'Nothing you can help me with, my dear.' He was smiling but again she could see beyond to the worry which lay just below the surface.

'Too bad you didn't inherit all that money old Mrs Foster left you,' he added, as he struggled into his coat. 'Things would have been very different. Oh, I am sorry, darling! My big mouth!' He bent to kiss her, and a moment later she was on her own.

Gradually the hard lump began to dissolve in her throat and the hot tears coursed down her cheeks. Then, in the silence of her empty house, Anna Cameron wept as she had never wept since the morning of old Mrs Foster's death.

Not even through all the accusations and the trial which went against her had she been able to weep with such abandon. She cried until she was tired, then slowly she sat up in her chair and poured herself a cup of tea, carrying it into the kitchen.

★ ★ ★

Once again she saw signs of neglect, but it didn't worry her any more. At one time, in her early nursing days, she had been unable to look at a smear of dirt without wanting to wipe it clean.

She had been a good nurse, with a sound, thorough training behind her in the early days of her marriage and she thought it had been very helpful to her as she brought up her family.

Then, when she found herself with time on her hands once more, and with Hugh needing every penny, she had been glad to take on the job of nursing old Mrs Foster of Sheldon Hall.

It was on the other side of town, but she could get a bus from door to door. And, besides, young Nurse Bell — Sharon Bell — was able to take over for night duty.

Where was Sharon now, Anna wondered, as she climbed the stairs and went into her bedroom. Hugh had kept this tidy. He had hung away his suits, and his shirts were neatly ironed and mended. Jill had done better for her father than she had done for herself! Yet — yet that neat patch on the front of Hugh's pale blue woollen shirt was not quite like Jill's work . . .

Thoughtfully, Anna unpacked her own case, pushing the plain blouses and skirts to the back of her wardrobe. Her nurse's uniform swung forward and she pushed it behind everything else.

She had been found guilty of betraying her trust, yet she had always considered herself innocent of everything. But was she truly innocent? Should she have depended upon Sharon Bell, who couldn't even tell the truth at the trial?

Yet, she and Sharon had exchanged duty for one another on a number of occasions. How was she to know that day would be so different?

Even as she stood at the open door of her wardrobe, she heard the front door opening and the sounds of footsteps in the hall, footsteps which faltered as they walked into the living-room.

'Mum?' Jill's voice was husky and uncertain, and Anna's feet were winged as she rushed downstairs.

'I'm here, darling.'

'Oh, Mum!' Jill cried, and a moment

later she was sobbing in her mother's arms. 'It — it's so strange to have you home again,' she said thickly, after she had wiped her eyes. There was so much to talk about that any awkwardness was soon dispelled.

'You never came to see me, darling,' said Anna after a while. 'You could have done, you know. It was an open prison.'

'I couldn't,' Jill cried. 'Oh, Mum, I couldn't see you in a place like that. Daddy said the time would pass, then it would seem as though you had never been away.'

'Then that's the way to think about it,' Anna replied soothingly. She had been hurt because her children had stayed away, but now she understood a little better.

'We'd better see about supper,' she announced briskly.

'Oh, Mum! It is just as though you've never been away,' Jill cried delightedly. 'When you said that, it was just like old times.'

'Of course it's just like old times!'

said a happy, young voice behind them, and Anna held out her arms to her only son and was enveloped in a bearlike hug.

'It's lovely to have you home again, Mum.'

'Put me down, Peter.' She laughed breathlessly.

Anna had been looking round her family as they all sat down to high tea.

'Myra hasn't called round yet,' she said. 'I half expected her to come after she picked the children up from school.'

'She's a busy girl,' Hugh defended when Jill and Peter made no reply, though Anna had caught the significant glance that had passed between them.

★   ★   ★

In the kitchen, Anna took pleasure in the simple task of washing the dishes, something she had once looked on as a chore. When she had finished, she had a look round the kitchen. Tomorrow, she would give it a really good going over, but tonight she was relishing the thought of a few quiet hours with her family.

When she went back to the sitting-room, though, Peter was putting on his jacket.

'Are you going out already?' Anna asked, disappointed.

'Yes, I'm meeting someone,' Peter replied, giving her a hug. And, with a casual wave of his hand, he was gone.

Anna turned to see Hugh getting to his feet.

'I'd better be off, too,' he said. 'I'm building a kitchen wall for John Findlay, and it has to be in the evenings, so that he can watch me every minute of the time.' He smiled ruefully at Anna as he made for the door. She held back from saying that, tonight of all nights, he could have arranged to be free.

After he'd gone, she switched on the television, but there was nothing she particularly wanted to see, so she picked up the embroidery she'd begun at Poplar Lodge.

All the time, though, she was listening with half an ear for the ring of the telephone. Surely Myra would phone . . .

Myra liked to have everything in her home well organised, a trait she'd inherited from her mother. She always fed Wendy and Paul at precisely five-thirty, although she and Charles often didn't eat till later as his hours were very flexible. He was the chief sales executive now for Foster & Davis and often worked late at night.

Old Mrs Foster's death had meant that a great deal of money and shares had gone to Roland Foster. No doubt the money, which Mrs Foster had intended for her, had also gone to him, thought Anna, with a small sigh. The firm must be in good heart at any rate. She wouldn't have wanted the money, though, even if circumstances had been different.

Throwing her embroidery aside, she went out into the hall and picked up the telephone.

After a moment, Myra's clear, light voice sounded in her ear and Anna's heart leapt. She and Myra sometimes had their differences, but she loved her eldest child dearly.

'Hello, my dear,' she said gently. 'This is Mum. I'm home at last. How are you all?'

She could hear the sudden intake of breath at the other end of the line and there was silence for a moment.

'Myra?' she said again. 'I rather thought you might have been round to see me, or to telephone at least — '

'You'll really have to excuse me, Mother,' Myra said in a high voice. 'I have visitors at the moment. I couldn't spare the time because I had everything to prepare for this evening, and now they're all just arriving. I'll have to go, Mother.'

'But . . . when can I see you, dear? I'm longing to see the children.'

'Look, I'll be in touch,' Myra said urgently. 'I'll give you a ring when I can, and I — I'll try to come and see you. I've got to go now. 'Bye.'

The receiver was slammed into place and Anna recoiled almost as though it had been a door slammed in her face.

Myra had sounded so strange, almost as though she were afraid that anyone would catch her talking to her mother!

Deeply hurt, Anna slowly returned to the living-room.

'Did you say your father was often home very late?' she asked Jill, who was watching television.

'Pretty late. So is Peter at times. He plays snooker and badminton to keep himself fit . . . or so he says! Shall I get us some cocoa, Mum?'

'Not for me, dear,' Anna said. 'I think I'll have a bath, then bed. It's been a — a long day.'

'Yes, I guess it must have been,' Jill said awkwardly. Was jail like hospital, the girl wondered — up at the crack of dawn each day? She couldn't ask her mother, not on her first day home.

Jill's own troubles crowded in on her as she switched off the TV programme.

What would her mother say when she learned she didn't want to carry on with her course at college? She had wanted to take up medicine, but how could she make any progress in such a career when her mother was convicted of causing death by neglect? Sooner or later, she was going to have to tell her mother.

Jill went into the kitchen, catching sight of her own bleak expression in the kitchen mirror. She blamed herself for what had happened to her mother. It was her fault that her mother had come home early that day, and had asked Sharon Bell to relieve her from duty at four instead of six.

Jill had been ill with a sore throat and Anna had always fussed over her since she had rheumatic fever as a child. Yet she couldn't help being ill. Sometimes, though, she wondered if Myra and Peter might blame her a little . . .

In spite of her mother's refusal, she carried a cup of steaming hot cocoa up to her parents' bedroom. Her mother was in the bath and Jill knocked loudly on the door.

'Cocoa beside your bed, Mum,' she called.

Anna's heart warmed.

'Thank you, darling,' she answered. 'I'll be out in a minute.'

★　★　★

Anna enjoyed her warm scented bath, and her spirits began to revive. It was many months since she had shared a bed with her husband, and on impulse she had folded away her rather mundane nightdress. Unzipping her pretty nightdress case, she lifted out a pale pink silk nightie trimmed with soft lace.

Both items had been a birthday gift from old Mrs Foster. At least, she had given Anna the money to buy the gift, and had insisted that Anna had spent the money as the old woman instructed.

As she pulled out the nightie, a small

box also fell at her feet, and Anna picked it up, throwing back the lid. It contained a pretty ring in an old-fashioned setting — another gift from Mrs Foster.

'It's for young fingers like yours, my dear Anna,' she said, 'not poor old knuckles like mine. Take it, my dear.'

'Oh, no, please!' Anna had protested. 'You've given me enough already. The nightie is gorgeous. I'm keeping it for a special occasion. Perhaps Hugh and I will have an exotic holiday one day!'

'Then this ring can also be for a special occasion, though you'd better have the stone fixed. It's a solitaire, and it's come a little bit loose from the setting. It's a pretty ring, but rather old, I'm afraid. My late husband gave it to me just after we were married. It belonged to his mother.'

'Then surely, Mrs Foster — your son's wife should have it.'

'She has plenty of rings, Anna dear, and will have more when I'm gone. No, I want you to have it.'

'But . . . isn't it valuable?' she asked. The stone was reasonably large, but rather dull. Anna had heard that zircons and spinels could look almost like diamonds. Perhaps it was one of those.

'Its value lies in seeing you enjoying it,' the old lady said. 'I've grown very fond of you, Anna. Your touch is very soothing, and my days pass so pleasantly when I have you to look after me. I like listening to your voice and hearing about your nice family. That's worth more than any ring.'

Anna had zipped the ring box into the nightdress case for convenience as she talked to the lady, but later she had forgotten all about it.

Her cocoa had grown a little cool, but Anna drank it gratefully, then settled down with a book to wait for Hugh. She heard Peter coming home, and his laughter mingling with Jill's as they came up to bed, but there was no sound of Hugh until after midnight.

She heard his soft footsteps on the stairs, then they retreated once more and the living-room door opened and shut very quietly. Then there was silence.

Then realisation dawned. Hugh wasn't coming up to their bedroom. He was spending the night on the bed-settee.

Deeply hurt, Anna lay for a long time with the bedside light still on. Then she reached out and clicked the room into darkness.

Downstairs, Hugh tossed and turned on the settee. It was reasonably comfortable, but he would have given much to be lying in his own bed upstairs. It had been very late when he finished that job for the Findlays. He was glad to take work other people turned down because of unsociable hours, and John Findlay was very pernickety about the work being done.

Pleased with the result of Hugh's labours, he had kept him talking and reminiscing about old times in Castleden. It had been late when Hugh left the Findlays' home and he didn't want to disturb Anna on her first night home. She must be very tired.

* ★ ★

Anna slept late the following morning and barely had time to get downstairs and put the kettle on before waking up her family. She often wondered where the hour between seven-thirty and eight-thirty went each morning. Peter and Jill had left before their father appeared.

Hugh was late in coming in for his breakfast, but when he did, he had already shaved and dressed.

'Hello, dear,' he said. 'So you're on duty again, I see. Sorry I was so late last night. I didn't want to wake you.'

'I wasn't asleep,' she said quietly.

The telephone shrilled and he strode into the hall to answer it. Anna could hear the high tones of a woman's voice on the other end of the line, then she watched Hugh stroking his chin.

'No, I can't discuss it now,' he said in a low tone. Again there was silence while the caller talked.

'Very well,' he agreed. 'I'll see you as

soon as I can. Yes, yes. I'll try to manage that.'

'Who was it?' Anna asked curiously.

'Work,' Hugh said briefly. 'I have to accept what work I can get these days, even if it means working at nights.'

'Then can't you sit down and drink a cup of morning tea with me?'

'Not possible,' he said hurriedly. 'It's even rare for me to eat breakfast these mornings. I must be available to see what I can get and said I would be at the office early this morning. I've tendered for repairs to the baker's in the High Street, and I need that job.'

'I see. I'm sorry you're having this worry, Hugh,' she said with sympathy. Almost before she knew it, he had quickly kissed her cheek, and the front door slammed, leaving the house silent.

Anna tidied up swiftly and efficiently. It would take some time to bring the house round to her ways, but she wasn't in a mood to start this morning. For one thing, she wanted to see Myra.

Jill said that she was holding a coffee

morning for Oxfam, but if Anna went to see her now, there would be plenty of time to talk before her guests arrived, and the children would be at home since the schools were closed for the Easter break.

Myra's house looked fresh and well cared for, even at the back entrance, as Anna took a short cut along a narrow path and approached the house through the back garden. She could hear the children's shrieking voices and their laughter as they played in the large kitchen.

Moments later she had pushed the door open.

There was a silence for a moment as two pairs of astonished eyes regarded her silently, then Wendy and Paul rushed towards her, almost knocking her to the floor in their eagerness.

It was the kind of welcome Anna had dreamed about!

'Granny!' Wendy cried. 'Where have you been? Mummy kept saying you'd gone away, and you didn't even come to my birthday party, and I wanted you. I missed you.'

'Missed you,' Paul echoed. 'Sweeties.'

'Cupboard love,' Anna said, settling herself down on a chair.

'Why didn't you come with Grandad?' Wendy was asking.

'Because I've been away,' Anna said.

'I mean now!' Wendy insisted.

Slowly, Anna became aware of the low murmur of voices in the sitting-room, and even as Wendy spoke, she thought she could detect the low timbre of Hugh's voice.

Slowly, she walked across the kitchen and opened the door into the hall, then crossed into the large, comfortable sitting-room.

Myra and Hugh were sitting side by side on the settee and so intent on each other's conversation that they did not see Anna.

'It's going to cause a lot of trouble, Dad.' Myra was saying. 'I think she must have it somewhere. There's no other explanation.'

'I'm Janet Fairbairn . . .'

'What's going to cause a lot of trouble?' Anna asked, as she walked into her daughter's sitting-room. 'Is it anything to do with me?'

Hugh and Myra looked round, startled.

'I thought you had to get to the office, Hugh,' Anna continued calmly, though there was a tightness in her throat. Myra hadn't wanted to see her when she got home, and now Anna suspected that she and Hugh were talking about her behind her back.

'Do you mind telling me what's going on?'

'You gave us a surprise, darling, that's all,' Hugh said as he leapt to his feet and pulled forward a deep armchair beside the fire. 'Sit down,' he invited.

But Anna's eyes were on her

daughter and a moment later Myra had run over to hug her mother.

'It's lovely to see you, Mum,' she said huskily, kissing her rather awkwardly on the cheek. 'How are you? Sit there and I'll get you a cup of coffee.'

'No need for that,' Anna said. 'I know you're having your coffee morning in a little while. I just wondered what was going on, that's all. I suspect it was you on the telephone to your father this morning, Myra?'

'Quite right,' she said airily. 'I only wanted to tell Father there are prospects of building repair work to be done at Foster & Davis's main office block, and Charles said that if he hurries over, he could tender for it straightaway. Charles doesn't think they'll want to waste too much time on estimates, so the job could be his if he wants it.'

'Wants it!' Hugh echoed. 'I want all the work I can get!'

'Oh . . . I see,' Anna said. But why did they seem to be making such a secret of it, she wondered.

'It's lovely to see the children again,' she said, settling down in the chair. 'They've both grown. I used to think Paul was quiet, but my word, he's come on in the past — past six months . . . ' Her voice tailed off and she bit her lip.

'They're a handful,' Myra said quickly, 'especially when they're on holiday from school. I'll have my work cut out until after Easter.'

'Perhaps I could help,' Anna said hopefully. 'You know it's no trouble to me to look after them. If you have to go out at any time, Myra, just give me a ring and I'll be pleased to sit with them. I feel I shall have to get to know them all over again.'

'Oh, I expect I'll manage, but thank you very much,' Myra said, smiling with difficulty. Anna saw her glancing once again at her father, and Hugh got to his feet.

'I'd better go now before my competitors get wind of this work at Foster & Davis. Come on, dear, and I'll drop you at the door as I go past. It'll 'save you a walk.'

'Yes, Mum, you do that,' Myra said, more warmly. 'You know I — I'm rather busy just now, but as soon as I'm free, I'll be round to see you. Promise.'

Anna's eyes softened. So often Myra had said just that very word to her, and she had always tried to keep her promises.

'Bring the children, dear,' she said gently. 'And Charles. It will be nice to see him again, too.'

'Yes.' Myra had withdrawn into herself again, and Hugh took Anna's arm as he guided her firmly to the car and settled her into her seat. It was only a short drive back round to their own house, but Anna had the uncomfortable feeling that she had been hustled out of Myra's house.

'Well, here we are, darling,' he said, drawing up at the gate. 'Oh, could you phone the office and say I won't be in until later in the afternoon?' He glanced at the car clock.

'I have another appointment after

Foster & Davis, so I'll just eat a sandwich out somewhere. I'll see to any calls when I do get back. OK?' he said.

'OK,' she replied automatically.

She searched in her handbag for her key, but her thoughts were still full of Myra and the tail-end of the conversation she had heard.

She must have it, Myra had been saying, there's no other explanation.

What must she have? She was sure the conversation referred to herself, whatever Myra said.

Taking off her coat, she set about bringing the house under her own control once more, and polishing it up to her own reasonably high standard. Yet her heart wasn't in it, thought Anna, even though she had often dreamed about this very moment as she lay down in bed each night while in prison.

★   ★   ★

Switching off her cleaner, Anna pushed back her hair and on impulse, picked up the telephone. She would ring one of her best friends, Muriel Falconer, who lived nearby. Unlike some of her so-called friends, Muriel had been kind enough to write to her at Poplar Lodge. If anyone could cheer her up, it would be Muriel.

She dialled the number and listened to the familiar ring of Muriel's telephone, then suddenly the warm, soft voice was in her ear so that she felt the prickle of tears behind her eyes.

'Muriel?' she asked huskily. 'It's Anna. I — I'm home.'

For a brief moment she heard the tell-tale intake of breath.

'I just thought I would ring,' she said quietly. 'I must break the ice some time.'

'Oh, no ice, Anna dear!' Muriel cried. 'Not with me! Would you — er — how would you like to come round for coffee?'

For a moment Anna hesitated, but the temptation was too much. It was another moment she had dreamed about.

'I would love to, Muriel. Thank you for asking me. I'll be with you in just a moment.'

Almost for the first time she really felt she had come home when she walked along the familiar path which linked their back gardens, and found Muriel with the kitchen door open ready for her.

'By the way, Anna, I think I'd better mention . . . Oh dear, here she comes now!'

There was a ring at the bell, and Muriel hurried to open the front door. A moment later Anna's smile faded as she heard Mrs Meldrum's voice in the hall.

'Sorry I'm a wee bit late, Muriel,' she was saying, 'but I've brought your collecting box with the flags for the old folk's outing. You take the town hall steps . . . Oh!'

She started visibly when she saw Anna sitting in front of the fire.

'Oh, it's you, Mrs Cameron,' she said stiffly.

Anna glanced at the clock. 'This is nice,' she said brightly. 'If I were still at Poplar Lodge, I would either be working in the laundry or maybe in the kitchens today.'

'I don't know how you can even talk about it, Mrs Cameron,' Ivy Meldrum said. 'I mean . . . even if it was an open prison, it's still prison.'

'Yes, I'm a jailbird, I suppose,' Anna said, and this time even Muriel coloured at her friend's frankness.

'What I can't understand is how you came to flush those drugs down the toilet,' Mrs Meldrum said, her eyes suddenly inquisitive. 'I mean, it seemed a silly thing to do, especially when some of the powder was spilled, or stuck to the sides. You know what I mean. The police are so clever these days about finding evidence like that. I would have thought you would know that, Mrs Cameron.'

Anna's cheeks had slowly reddened with inner anger.

'It's quite simple, Mrs Meldrum, and

I'm surprised you don't realise it! I didn't flush any drugs down the toilet, and I said so repeatedly at the trial . . . '

'But the evidence — it was all there. It all came out, didn't it?'

'I agree it might have looked that way but I still didn't do it!'

'Of course she didn't, Ivy!' Muriel cried.

'I read the papers every day,' Mrs Meldrum argued. 'I know what was said.'

'I think I'd better go, Muriel,' Anna said, getting to her feet. 'I've got such a lot to do in the house. It's been a bit neglected.'

'Yes, I know how it is,' Muriel agreed almost too readily, so that Anna lost no time in putting on her coat.

'Don't mind Ivy,' Muriel whispered at the door. 'Some people just don't understand.'

'No, I don't suppose they do,' Anna said sadly.

★ ★ ★

How empty and cheerless her home seemed when she returned once more, and how angry she felt with Ivy Meldrum. If only she could knock the truth into the woman's head! Yet how could she convince Mrs Meldrum about what really happened on that terrible day when she couldn't understand it herself? Nor could she convince a jury that she was telling the truth.

She sat down at the kitchen table and put her head in her hands. She had thought about it so often, going over the evidence in her mind, knowing that Sharon Bell must be hiding something.

She had prepared the drugs for Sharon to give Mrs Foster at six o'clock precisely. It was essential that the old lady got the full dosage at the exact time each day, and Anna had always given her the drugs as she was going off duty.

'Last job of the day, Anna,' Mrs Foster had said so many times, and obediently put out her tongue so that the white powder could be put at the back of it. She often said she had been given her medicine in just this fashion by her nanny when she was a little girl, and liked to take it best this way. Afterwards, she drank a glass of iced water.

Anna had measured out the drugs, and had left them on the medicine tray for Sharon to administer. She had told Mrs Foster she was going off duty early, and Sharon would relieve her at four o'clock instead of six.

'I've telephoned Nurse Bell,' she said. 'I must go home, Mrs Foster. It's Jill. She's developed a very bad throat again and I've just telephoned home to ask about her. Hugh thinks her temperature has gone up. I'll have to get the doctor. I'm so afraid for her, in case she has another bout of rheumatic fever.'

'That's all right, dear,' Mrs Foster whispered. 'Don't you worry.'

'I'll wait for Nurse Bell. She should be coming on duty at four o'clock, then I can go home.'

'Go now, Anna.'

'Not until Sharon arrives,' she said firmly.

But the worry of Jill was uppermost in her mind, and as the hands of the clock crept round the last few minutes towards four o'clock, which was the earliest time Sharon would manage to reach Sheldon Hall, Anna felt herself tightening up with nerves.

'Just run along, my dear,' Mrs Foster said again. 'I'll be fine. My son might look in soon, or my grandson. I'll just take a little nap and Nurse Bell will be here in a few minutes.'

'Well . . . if you're sure,' Anna said. 'I've left everything ready for her. I'll write her a little note.'

Quickly she scribbled the note on the back of an old envelope, then left it propped up near the medicine tray. A moment later she was struggling into her coat, then she turned and waved to Mrs Foster. It was the last time she had seen the old lady alive.

What had happened? Anna Cameron wondered for the thousandth time.

Nurse Bell had denied everything. She hadn't seen any note. She hadn't been asked to come in early. She hadn't administered the drugs, presuming that Nurse Cameron would have done that when she left at six o'clock, though she had been surprised not to meet Nurse Cameron leaving the house as she arrived. It was a rule that they always waited for one another.

'But Nurse Cameron says you often did extra duty for one another,' her counsel had stated. 'Would you not agree this was so, Nurse Bell?'

'No, it was most unusual for the routine to be changed,' Sharon had declared. She had refused to meet Anna's eyes, no doubt because of the accusation she might have seen.

They had often exchanged an hour of duty. It had worked very well in the past. Why had it not worked on this occasion?

Sharon had obviously tried to destroy the drugs by flushing them down the toilet, and in her nervousness she had spilled some of them. That had added to the evidence against Anna.

But who would believe her now, she wondered. She had thought her friends would know she was far from being so irresponsible. Yet Ivy Meldrum had believed Sharon's evidence. The prosecution had accused Anna of depriving Mrs Foster of the drugs, knowing that her life could be ended.

But she had not known such a thing. She would have expected Mrs Foster to become rather weaker if deprived of her drugs for a few hours, but she would never have expected her to die. She would have expected her to rally as soon as the next dose was administered and perhaps to be rather more ill for a day or two.

She hadn't known that the old woman was now so very weak. Old Dr Meredith called every day, but he had not expressed an opinion that the old lady was so near death . . .

★　★　★

40

The door suddenly flew open and Peter stood there, grinning broadly.

'Peter! Am I glad to see you!' she cried, laughing to stifle the sob in her throat.

'Hello, Mum! I hope you're not too busy. I'm going over to Thornbank on a job, and I wondered if you'd like to sit in with me. I've got one of the firm's cars at the door.'

'Oh, Peter,' she said, her eyes shining. 'I'd love to drive to Thornbank with you. I could do with a nice change like that.'

She was ready in no time and Peter proudly escorted her towards a gleaming white car which stood at the gate.

'I'm saving up for my own car, Mum, but I doubt if it will be one like this,' he enthused.

'Have your father and Myra been worrying about anything recently?' she asked, as they drove along. 'She was on the telephone this morning, then later he went round to see her. She said it was a building repair job at Foster & Davis.'

'Probably it was,' Peter said. 'He'll be glad of a job at Foster & Davis. Young Mr Foster has just returned from America and he'll be making things hum. I expect that's why there's a repair job already. He checks up on everything. Do you remember Stephen Foster, Mum?'

'I certainly do,' Anna bit her lip. He was old Mrs Foster's grandson and he and his smart young wife had visited the old lady from time to time. But always he had brought an air of impatience into the sick room. His wife, too, had always been restless and showed all too easily her relief when they were due to leave once more, their duty to the old lady finished for another day.

'How are you, Grandmother?' Stephen would ask.

'Well, since you ask, I'd be a lot better off dead!' she would say, though her eyes would twinkle a little as they met Anna's.

'Don't say that, Grandmother!'

Stephen would say.

'Why not? It's the truth.'

But it had always been said ruefully. Mrs Foster loved life and would never have wanted to end it before her time came.

Stephen Foster had told the police that his grandmother had made this statement on more than one occasion, and when Anna was questioned she always maintained that the old lady hadn't said it seriously.

'Did you agree to help her end her life?' she had been asked. 'Was the money she left you reward for doing this?'

'Certainly not. She would never have asked me to do such a thing. I didn't know she would leave me any money.'

The echo of her own voice rang in her ears, and Stephen Foster's accusing eyes seemed to stare into her own. He had believed her guilty of everything — now he was home and playing a major part in running the firm, even if he was still the junior partner.

How would this affect Charles, Myra's husband? Old Mr Foster had always been kind and considerate to Anna. But things might change with Mr Stephen now in power.

'Here we are at Thornbank,' Peter announced happily. 'I often have to drive to neighbouring towns like this,' he added.

'I'm so glad you're enjoying your work, my dear,' she said gently. 'No girlfriends yet?'

'Quite a few and — well — I did meet one girl I liked when I had to investigate some damage to property in March. But I've only seen her once or twice since.' Peter blushed a little. 'Her name is Elizabeth, but that's all I know about her really. She's a nice girl, though. She's in Edinburgh at the moment, but she said she might be back in Castleden after Easter. I shan't be long. I'll switch on the radio for you.'

She listened to the radio, then nodded off to sleep for a while. Peter was taking his time, she thought, when she woke.

Suddenly Peter had returned to the car, his young face alert and a smile on his lips as he slid into the driver's seat.

'Sorry, it took longer than I had expected. The shop had an alarm bell, but the thieves got away with a load of stuff, even though the bell went off.'

Anna was glad that she had so little time to prepare dinner after she got home. It was nice to be busy enough not to be a clock-watcher once more, she thought.

The table had been set, and Anna remembered that she had some pretty table napkins in the sideboard drawer. She was rummaging through a variety of accumulated objects when suddenly the kitchen door opened and a youngish woman walked in.

'Hello!' she called. 'Are you in, Hugh?'

Slowly Anna pushed the drawer shut, her whole attention being given to the attractive woman who stood in the middle of the kitchen floor, a laundry box in her hands, as she looked round for a likely spot to put it down.

Anna recognised one or two of Hugh's shirts, and the pale grey and bottle green sweater which lay at the top of the box. It was one she had bought for his birthday a year ago.

'Mr Cameron isn't home yet,' she said, walking through into the kitchen.

The woman jumped with shock as Anna appeared in the doorway.

'Oh!' she cried. 'I — I suppose you're Mrs Cameron. We haven't met, but I'm Janet Fairbairn, I work for Hugh. I expected him to be back to the office, but it looks as though he's not going to return this afternoon. I — er — I've been helping him with his laundry while you — while you were away.'

Another Kind Of Prison

It took Anna a moment to recover from the shock of seeing a young woman looking so much at home in her own kitchen. She held out her hand rather awkwardly.

'How do you do, Miss Fairbairn? I . . . I'm afraid my husband didn't mention . . . but we have a lot of catching up to do.'

'His last assistant left to get married,' Janet Fairbairn explained, equally ill-at-ease. She still held the box of laundry in her hands, and Anna hurried forward to take it from her.

'Here, let me take that. It . . . it's really very kind of you . . . Oh, here's Hugh now!'

The car had drawn up at the gate and both women sighed inwardly with relief. A moment later Hugh had walked into the house with his long, purposeful stride, pausing with surprise when he saw Janet Fairbairn.

'I brought your laundry,' she explained hastily. 'When I didn't hear, I presumed you wouldn't be coming back to the office this afternoon.'

'I've just looked in there,' he explained, then turned to Anna. 'Didn't you make that telephone call, my dear?'

It was Anna's turn to blush.

'Oh dear, I'll have to write everything down until I get used to being back. I must apologise, darling. I completely forgot.'

'No harm done,' Hugh said easily. 'We've got the contract for Foster & Davis, Janet, and I've also been to see Hughes in High Street. But they've postponed any alterations to their premises for this year. So it's good news and bad news.'

Janet Fairbairn was smiling at Hugh.

'I'm delighted about Foster & Davis,' she enthused.

Looking on, Anna had the strange feeling of being shut out. She hadn't seen Hugh looking so animated since before . . . before she went to prison. She felt a sharp pang of unease — surely there was more in Janet Fairbairn's look than mere admiration and respect for her employer . . .

Anna pulled herself together.

'Would you care to stay and share our meal, Miss Fairbairn?' she asked. 'It's almost ready and our son and daughter will be home very soon. It would be no trouble to set one more place. In fact, here's Peter now.'

'Oh no, thank you, Mrs Cameron. I mustn't stay any longer,' Janet Fairbairn told her hurriedly. 'I live with my mother, and I help to prepare our meal each evening. She is a little bit handicapped by arthritis, you see.'

'I'm sorry,' Anna replied, but even as Janet moved towards the door, Jill, too, had returned home. Anna noticed that although her children greeted Janet Fairbairn politely there was an air of constraint between them. She watched as Hugh showed his secretary to the door and continued talking animatedly to her as they walked down the path. Then he turned with a wave of the hand and came back to join his family.

'I'm glad you got that contract, darling,' Anna said cheerfully.

'It certainly is a great relief to me,' said Hugh. Now that Janet had gone, he was once again the rather quiet man she knew, with the faint frown of worry between his eyes.

'I went out with Peter this afternoon,' she told the family. 'It's been fun. How are things with you, Jill?'

'All right,' Jill said laconically.

At one time Jill had chattered continuously about school and her plans for the future. But she wasn't so forthcoming any more, her mother thought.

'I'm going out to play badminton, Mum,' she said. 'I don't want very much to eat.'

'I'll have your share,' said Peter. 'I'm going out as well, Mum.'

'Well, don't be too late either of you,'

Anna said automatically. 'Remember you both have to get up in the morning.'

⋆ ⋆ ⋆

Over the next week or two Anna Cameron made a valiant effort to settle down once again in the community, but Castleden was a small town with a long memory. There would be talk for a long time to come and gradually she found herself making excuses to stay in and asking Jill to do the shopping.

'I haven't much time at the lunch hour, Mum,' Jill protested when Anna asked her to bring a card of buttons home for her newest blouse. 'Aren't you going shopping yourself today? I never seem to choose the right shade of buttons to suit you.'

'I'll give you a piece of material. Surely you can match it up. I can't go myself because I've decided to give the utility room a coat of paint . . . '

'All right, Mum, I'll choose your

buttons for you.' Jill's tone was brusque and Anna looked at her closely — her daughter had never before been impatient with her like that.

Anna sighed and tied a scarf round her hair. It was a relief to find an excuse to stay at home. She was becoming tired of keeping up her courage. She had only been painting for a short time when Myra called to see her, and Anna laid aside her brush with delight — Myra's visits were very rare.

'I'm sorry,' Myra said awkwardly. 'I see I've picked a fine day to come!'

'Any day suits me.' Anna laughed. 'Just let me get rid of this paint and we can have some coffee.'

'I'll get it,' said Myra, and her mother smiled happily. So often Myra merely paid a flying visit, then made some excuse to get away again as quickly as she possibly could.

'This is nice,' Anna said, plumping herself down on her favourite kitchen chair. 'How are the children?'

'Fine at the moment,' said Myra. She

moved restlessly and her mother could see she wasn't at ease.

'Is there something wrong?' she asked.

'I . . . there is something bothering Charles and me, Mum, and I'm sorry I have to ask you about it. I came round specially when . . . when I thought you might be on your own.' Myra's voice was halting and her eyes distressed.

'What's wrong?' Anna asked quietly.

'I'm sorry to have to ask, but did old Mrs Foster ever give you any presents, Mum?'

Anna's eyes widened. 'Indeed she did! She gave me a lovely nightdress for my birthday — it was a kindly thought. She wanted me to wear it when I went on holiday. Why do you ask?'

'I don't mean that sort of present, Mum,' Myra said impatiently. Her manner was much more brisk now that the ice had been broken. 'I mean something much more valuable than a nightie . . . '

'More valuable!' cried Anna, her face

going pale. 'What do you mean, Myra, and why are you asking these questions?'

'It's Stephen Foster, Mum, not me. He . . . he says there's something missing from Mrs Foster's room . . . '

'How dare he!' Anna leapt to her feet. 'What have I ever done to him! He's tried every way to blacken my name and even gave evidence against me. Is he now accusing me of taking valuables from an old lady? Do you believe I would do that, Myra?'

'Oh, Mum! Of course not, but I know he's going to ask you about it.'

'Let him!' cried Anna. 'I should like to have a talk with Mr Foster face to face. He knows very well I looked after his grandmother as though she were my own . . . my own . . . '

Anna's eyes filled and Myra leapt to her feet.

'Don't upset yourself, Mum,' she said impatiently. 'I can see there's some mistake somewhere. Anyway, I had to ask. I'd better go now and let you get on with your painting.'

Was there to be no end to her worries over old Mrs Foster? Anna asked herself as she watched Myra pick up her bag and make for the kitchen door.

'What sort of valuables is he talking about?' she called after her daughter.

'Jewellery, I think . . . something like that,' Myra replied. 'I'll see myself out.'

Anna sat motionless at the kitchen table after Myra had gone. Surely old Mrs Foster's jewellery had been kept in the bank. It would have been handed over to her son, Roland, when she died.

With a heavier heart Anna once again picked up her paintbrush and began to attack the walls of the utility room.

* * *

Jill was first home, wrinkling her nose at the smell of paint. 'It'll taste my food,' she complained.

'Well, it has to be done,' her mother told her. 'That utility room was like a

55

dungeon. There's a letter for you, by the way.'

Jill turned scarlet.

Anna watched curiously while she slit it open and began to read.

She turned to her mother with a look of mingled excitement and defiance on her face.

'What is it, dear?' asked Anna.

'It's . . . I've got a job, Mum.'

'A job!' Anna's mouth opened with surprise. 'But . . . what do you mean . . . a job? I thought you wanted to go to university . . . study Medicine.'

'I don't want to take any more examinations, Mum, and I don't want to do Medicine. I've decided I want to be a telephone operator, and I've been accepted for training. I've already got all the qualifications I need.'

Anna's head began to ache. Hadn't she had enough for one day?

'Bring that oval plate through to the table, Jill,' she invited. 'I've baked a cutting cake and you can put out a few slices. I think we'll have to talk this over with your father. You've always wanted to take up Medicine. It's what I should like to have done myself, but in my days things were different.'

Jill said nothing. Her face had a closed look as she cut the cake.

'Jill?'

'There's nothing to discuss, Mum. I've made up my mind. I can do what I like with my own life.'

'But you're very young, my dear. I don't want you to make a mistake.'

'It wasn't I who made the mistake, Mum,' Jill snapped suddenly, and there was a sparkle of angry tears in her eyes. 'What chance have I at medical school when my mother was convicted of causing death by neglect? What sort of reception do you think I'd get if I applied for training? It's bad enough already at school.

'That's why . . . why I want to be a telephonist. At least I'll only be a voice at the other end of the phone. I don't have to give my . . . my name . . . ' Her voice choked then faded into silence.

Anna stood as though turned to stone. It was Jill . . . her beloved Jill . . . who was saying these terrible things. Yet it was a Jill who must have been hurt badly. Young people could be cruel to one another, and she could imagine how Jill would suffer from the raised eyebrows and the stifled giggles. But surely she wouldn't be penalised in her career because of her mother? Surely not in this day and age!

'Have you tried — ' she began.

'I don't want to discuss it any more,' Jill cried.

Suddenly the door flew open and Peter strode into the room, his eyes blazing angrily.

'And you won't talk to our mother like that!' he snapped. 'I don't know what this is all about, but I've been watching your sulks ever since Mum came home, Jill, and it's high time you heard a few home truths. If Mum hadn't put you before everything on the day Mrs Foster died, none of this would have happened.'

'Peter! Jill!' There was a shrill note in Anna's voice.

Jill quickly picked up her bag and her letter, then ran upstairs. They heard the slam of her bedroom door.

'Let her go, Mum,' said Peter quietly. 'She'll just have to come round in her own good time.'

Anna drew a shuddering breath. What was happening to her family, and her home? It was turning into another kind of prison cell, instead of a place of warmth and love.

★   ★   ★

Jill was shamefaced next morning when she came down to breakfast. She apologised to her mother and received a bearlike hug from Peter.

'That's more like our Jill,' Peter said as she pushed him away.

Anna could see there was still quite a lot of reserve in her.

'I still want to take this job, Mum,' she said, as she ate her toast and marmalade. 'I think I would enjoy it.'

'What job?' asked Hugh, coming into the kitchen.

Jill glanced at the clock and leapt to her feet.

'Mum will tell you,' she said. 'I've got to rush now, Dad.'

'What job?' he repeated, as Jill banged the front door, and Peter followed her a moment or two later.

'I was going to tell you last night, but you were late again,' said Anna, rather wearily.

'Yes, I had to finish some estimates and took them round to Janet's for typing. Then old Mrs Fairbairn wanted to show me some of her ancient photographs. She doesn't get out much, so I felt I had to stay with her for a little while.'

'Perhaps I could go and see her sometime,' Anna said thoughtfully. 'She would always be someone to talk to during the day.'

'I'll see what Janet says,' Hugh promised and this time Anna's eyes darkened. She was beginning to hear that phrase quite a lot!

'Jill wants to take a job as a telephonist,' she said. 'The only reason she wants it is so that she can hide away from people. She doesn't want to do Medicine any more because of . . . of me.'

'I see,' said Hugh, after a long pause.

'You talk to her, darling,' Anna said coaxingly. 'You've always been able to talk to Jill. At least she could try to take up Medicine. It's what she has always wanted to do.'

'She might be even more hurt if she tries and is turned down!'

'I don't agree!' Anna replied emphatically.

Hugh paused, then kissed her briefly on the forehead.

'It's sad, but true, that the rest of us have served that sentence with you, Anna. Now, don't look like that! I'm not blaming you! But it's true, nevertheless. It affects all of us, dear.' His words were like pinpricks, even if he did not realise it.

Anna watched him picking up his coat.

'I shan't be back to lunch,' he said. 'I'll have a sandwich out today.'

'Very well.' She nodded, and once again, as the door closed, the hated silence of the house was all around her, and she had to switch on the radio so that she could hear the sound of another human voice. Anna spent the morning tidying her bedroom and putting the laundry back into the drawers. She had washed the pretty nightdress Mrs Foster had given her, and she slipped it carefully into the matching case.

Suddenly her fingers closed once more on the old ring box containing the ring the old lady had insisted she accept. It had slipped her mind again, and Anna flicked back the lid and looked at the pretty stone in its heavy setting which looked like solid silver, though the shank was probably gold. One or two of the claws had worn and were no longer holding the stone in place. It was rather dull, but when she looked at it closely and rubbed it with a tissue, it glowed attractively.

For a moment Anna frowned, remembering Myra's visit. Surely she hadn't meant this ring! Surely Mr Stephen Foster couldn't be anxious about this small piece of jewellery! It was hardly valuable. How could he be so mean as to pursue the whereabouts of a ring which had been a gift to her?

Anna tried it on her finger and in her mind's eye she could see old Mrs Foster beaming at her with approval. The old lady had wanted her to wear it. Carefully she slipped it back into its case, then placed it in her handbag, deciding to call in at Davidson's in the High Street. Perhaps they could strengthen the setting for her.

An hour later she reached Davidson's, wishing she'd had the sense to call there first. That way she wouldn't have had a heavy shopping bag to carry around. Wearily she put it down at her feet on the luxurious carpet and handed over the ring in its box to old Mr Davidson.

* * *

'It was a gift,' Anna explained, 'but the setting needs to be secured, and you can see that two claws are rather worn, Mr Davidson.'

'Take a seat, Mrs Cameron,' the old man invited, eyeing her over his half-spectacles. 'I need an eyeglass for this job. Now just let me look . . . '

Anna was glad to sit down. Her eyes roamed all over the shop, admiring the showcases of fine silver and charming pieces of modern jewellery.

Mr Davidson was taking his time. He had called his son, Mark, through from the back of the shop and now they were both examining the ring.

'I should say it's at least eight carats, but we would have to measure it,' said Mark.

'Set in heavy silver, with a gold shank. Antique value as well . . . '

Slowly Anna rose to her feet.

'What kind of stone is it, Mr Davidson?' she asked. 'I've heard that a zircon or a spinel can be that colour . . . '

'You don't know?' asked old Mr Davidson, coming to peer at her closely. 'You say it was a gift, Mrs Cameron?'

She bit her lip.

'Yes. From . . . from a friend. She's dead now . . . She wanted me to wear it, but as you see, I was afraid I would lose the stone out of the setting. It's dull, but I thought it was pretty.'

'It's a very fine diamond, Mrs Cameron,' said Mr Davidson quietly. 'A very fine stone, indeed.'

She stared at him, her eyes going to Mark Davidson.

'Do you mean . . . ? Could it be valuable?'

Mr Davidson glanced at his son.

'It would not be easy to put an exact figure on it. Such fine jewellery isn't so easy to sell these days, but in London you could probably get fifteen thousand

pounds for it. Replacement value
... though there again it would be
difficult to make such a fine setting
these days ... replacement value would
probably be around twenty thousand
pounds.'

'It's Not Mine To Sell'

Anna remembered Myra's visit and her cheeks burned. It must be this ring which Stephen Foster had been asking about. He would know its value. Yet she had assured Myra that old Mrs Foster had never given her anything valuable!

'The ring will require to be re-set in order to ensure the safety of the stone, Mrs Cameron,' Mr Davidson added. 'Do you wish us to undertake this task?'

She came out of her reverie.

'Oh, yes, please. Er . . . I'll leave it with you then, Mr Davidson.'

'I'll send you a card when the repair has been carried out,' he promised, and once again she picked up her heavy shopping bag. But this time she hardly noticed its weight.

As soon as she got home, Anna dialled Myra's number, but there was no answer. She couldn't wait to be rid of the responsibility of the expensive ring.

Hugh walked in as she was trying to reach Myra for the third time.

'I thought she'd be back from picking Wendy up from school,' Anna said worriedly. 'I must get hold of her.'

'What's wrong now?' Hugh asked rather wearily.

'It's a ring old Mrs Foster gave me. You remember it, don't you, Hugh? It has a clear stone in the centre.'

'I remember.'

'Well, that clear stone is a diamond. It's worth at least fifteen thousand pounds. I'll have to return it to the Fosters.'

'Fifteen thousand pounds!' Hugh echoed.

'Yes, and if I'm not very careful, Stephen Foster will be accusing me of taking the ring. He's already been asking Myra about it, but I had no idea it was at all valuable until I took it to Mr Davidson to have it re-set.'

'Well, we certainly don't want more

trouble, Anna,' Hugh said coolly. 'Perhaps it's a pity you didn't have it valued earlier. We've got enough trouble already.'

'What do you mean?' Anna asked, puzzled by Hugh's attitude.

'Fosters appear to have changed their mind about the contract for their main building. Old Mr Foster has gone into hospital and Mr Stephen doesn't want to spend any money at the moment — or perhaps he's had second thoughts about employing Hugh Cameron. And that's not all. I tendered for repairs to Joseph Reid's at the thread mills and it went to Bob McNinch, yet my firm has always been employed by Reid's. It isn't hard to get the picture,' he ended, his eyes sliding away from her.

'You mean you think it's because of me?' Anna asked bluntly.

Hugh sighed, then his mouth twisted wryly.

'What does it matter? It's the end result which counts.'

'I'm sorry, darling,' Anna whispered

and bent to kiss his cheek, but he was turning away to reach for his paper.

She straightened and walked through to the kitchen to unpack the shopping she had carried home

Anna was so deep in thought that she scarcely noticed Jill's arrival home from school.

'Can you set out the cutlery, dear?' Anna asked. 'I really must try to telephone Myra again.'

'She was going to some sort of meeting with Charles,' Jill informed her mother. 'I saw her this afternoon when we were going to the playing fields. She'd just had her hair done.'

'Oh, I see.'

It was a fairly silent meal.

Jill sighed. Had she upset her parents so much by wanting to leave school straightaway? Her headmistress had also talked to her and had shown her the good sense of obtaining her 'A'-levels before leaving.

'You might want these qualifications one day, Jill,' she had said, 'then it will be so much harder to work for them. It seems a shame not to pick the fruit when it is almost ripe.'

'All right,' Jill had promised. 'I'll do all my exams before I leave.'

Now she cleared her throat and Anna looked up.

'I just wanted to tell you both that — that I'll go on at school and try to get through my exams,' she said. 'Though I want to be free to choose my own career after that.'

'That's a splendid idea,' her mother said warmly. 'Isn't it, Hugh?'

'Of course,' he agreed readily. 'That sounds fine, Jill.'

Jill offered her cup to be refilled, but it was all rather an anti-climax. Her parents had always seemed to care so much about her future. Did they still care?

She washed up while Anna borrowed the car for an hour.

Without saying anything to Hugh, she drove to Stephen Foster's home and asked to see Mr and Mrs Foster.

But the elderly house-keeper informed her that they were away on a trip to London, and Anna could only leave a message that she had called.

What a difference a sum like £15,000 would make to Hugh's business, she told herself the next day after Hugh left early for work. And it was hers by rights. Mrs Foster had given it to her as a gift.

Anna stared temptation in the face, then put it behind her. She would never have accepted the ring had she known it was so valuable. She did not want it, especially in view of the fact that Stephen Foster had been enquiring for it through Myra.

Myra! Anna got to her feet to go and telephone when it rang shrilly. Picking up the receiver she heard Muriel Falconer's voice at the other end.

'Hello, Anna? How do you feel about helping me at our bring and buy sale for the Red Cross?'

Anna's breath caught in her throat. Could she do such a thing? Muriel's bring and buy sales were always well attended, and she was bound to meet most of her old friends there.

'It would only be an hour, or maybe two, out of your time,' Muriel coaxed.

'Oh, I have plenty of time,' Anna said rather drily. 'Very well. When will you want me?'

'Come round here at half past nine. We've got to lay out the stalls at the church hall. You can help with that.'

Again Jill only had a brief glimpse of her mother as she and Peter came down rather late for breakfast.

Anna looked animated and excited as she changed into a smart suit.

'I'll be back for lunch, darling,' she said to Jill. 'We can have a salad, if that suits Peter.'

'I'll be out for lunch, Mum,' Peter said. 'I'm playing tennis. Mixed doubles. I hope I get a decent partner.'

'Your partner deserves better, too,' Jill said, and Peter aimed a mock blow at her.

★   ★   ★

Silently, Jill washed up the breakfast dishes, then started with fright as the doorbell shrilled loudly through the empty house. Quickly she smoothed down her curls, then went to open the door.

A tall, young man stood on the doorstep, his fair, curly hair ruffling gently in the wind.

'Yes?' she asked. 'Can I help you?'

'Er . . . Mrs Cameron, please,' he said hesitantly, and watched a withdrawn expression appear on Jill's face as she stepped back. Perhaps he was a reporter. There had been several at the door when Anna was sent to prison.

'Mrs Cameron is not at home,' she said firmly.

'Oh, well then, could I leave a message?' the young man asked hurriedly. 'My name is Adrian Scott. My grandfather is Dr Scott, a — a friend of Mrs Cameron's. He wishes me to return a book which she lent him. Also — '

'I'll be happy to take the book,' Jill

interrupted, a wary look still on her face as she held out her hand.

'I — well — I'd rather like to talk to a member of her family,' Adrian said quickly. 'Do you think I might come in for a moment?'

Jill paused. She had learned to be wary of everyone who called to see her mother. Once again she met his anxious blue eyes, unaware of how much he was able to read in her own small face with its drooping, vulnerable mouth and wide, brown, troubled eyes.

'Please come in,' she invited rather grudgingly, then her natural manners rose to the surface. 'I was just going to make a cup of coffee. Would you like some?'

'I'd love some, but only if I'm allowed to help.'

He looked very much at home as he sat in a chair near the fireplace, after placing the book on the kitchen table.

'It's about local history,' he explained. 'My grandfather is a fanatic and I think he shared that interest with Mrs Cameron.'

'My mother. I'm Jill Cameron.'

'My grandfather was old Mrs Foster's doctor,' Adrian Scott explained. 'I expect you remember. He's very concerned to find out how Mrs Cameron is. He's in poor health now, I'm afraid, otherwise he would have returned the book himself. He never thought — I mean, he always held your mother in high regard.'

'How kind of him,' Jill said crisply.

Once again her lips were pursed and Adrian Scott could see how much she disliked any mention of her mother's past trouble. She held out a plate of biscuits and he accepted one with thanks.

'What do you do with your life?' he asked, smiling.

'I'm doing my 'A'-levels,' Jill answered with a shrug.

'And after that?'

'I haven't decided yet.'

'What about a break from your studies then?' Adrian suggested. 'Do you play tennis or badminton?'

'I prefer not to go out much these

days.' Jill's face was closed again, but he could see the quiver of her mouth as she turned away. 'Please tell Dr Scott that my mother's fine and there's nothing for him to worry about.'

Adrian felt himself to be dismissed as he put down his coffee cup. Once again his eyes were on Jill's face. Was she fighting shy of going out amongst other young people? He hesitated as she walked forward to open the door.

'Please . . . Can't I see you again? Perhaps you share your mother's interest in local history? My grandfather says there are one or two old Roman sites in the area. He has a map and I've often thought I'd like to investigate some of the places he's marked. But it would be much more fun with you for company.'

Jill hesitated.

'Please come,' Adrian Scott insisted.

'We don't really know one another,' she objected.

'All the more reason why we should go. How about this afternoon at three o'clock? I'll pick you up in my car — it's not exactly a limousine but it'll get us there.'

A smile lit Jill's eyes. 'All right,' she agreed. 'I'll come.'

★ ★ ★

When Anna arrived home from the bring and buy sale, she found that Jill had already prepared lunch and there was a brightness to her which had been lacking.

Her own morning had also been bright with new promise and for once it had seemed as though she had never been away from Castleden as she helped to sell cakes, scones and biscuits.

Even the atmosphere in her home seemed lighter as Jill prepared to go out on a date, the first she'd had since her mother came home. And how nice it was that the young man was Dr Scott's grandson!

Then Peter rushed in to change into

his best trousers and new jacket, after a bath which had the walls of the bathroom running with steam.

'My word, but you're determined to cut a dash!' Anna laughed. 'Who's the lucky lady?'

'My partner in the mixed doubles,' Peter said rather shyly. 'Her name's Elizabeth Caldwell — I've met her before. She works in a bank and has just come back to Castleden from Edinburgh. She's a nice girl, Mum.'

'Bring her home for supper,' she invited, and Peter's eyes gleamed with laughter as he smiled to his mother.

'No fear,' he said. 'I've only just got to know her. I'm not going to rush her, Mum.'

'No, I suppose not,' said Anna.

She tidied the bathroom thoughtfully. What would happen when the time came for Peter to bring his girlfriend home? Sooner or later she would learn that Peter's mother had been in prison. Anna drew a deep breath. Why should she worry about that? Any girl who fell in love with Peter was surely the most fortunate girl in the world. It would not matter to her that his mother had been in prison if she loved Peter enough.

But some girls did care very deeply about that sort of thing. Myra, her own daughter, cared. Myra showed how much she cared by her every gesture, every turn of the head. Always it was her father she consulted now over family matters and she didn't seem to care that by doing so she was cutting Anna to the quick.

Anna had tried to talk this over with Hugh, but even he didn't appear to think it important. At one time, he seemed to appreciate her feelings and her needs so much better, thought Anna sadly.

She wandered into her bedroom. Perhaps Hugh could be persuaded to go out for the evening as they had once done on Saturdays. She looked into his wardrobe and lifted out his best dark suit, brushing it carefully. Then she searched amongst her own clothes and selected a pretty, soft pink silk suit, holding it up against herself. She was not quite as thin as she had been when she was first released from prison — the suit should fit her perfectly now.

Carefully, Anna laid out Hugh's clothes, then had a leisurely bath and changed into the pink suit. She found grey shoes and handbag, and her heart was light as she examined her reflection in her dressing-table mirror. In spite of all that she had gone through, there were few signs of it in her general appearance. Perhaps there were one or two grey hairs sprinkled amongst the fair curls, but her eyes still sparkled with life.

Anna waited for half an hour, then decided to walk round to the office and try to winkle Hugh away from his desk. Just for once, it would do him good to have a break.

It was growing dusky as she neared the office and she could see that the place was well lit with strip lighting.

Janet Fairbairn was sitting at her

desk, her fingers flying over her typewriter keys. How hard she worked for Hugh, thought Anna. No wonder he appreciated her efforts.

As she walked up the path towards the office, she could see Janet removing the letter from her typewriter and handing it to Hugh. As he took it, he also took Janet's hand in his.

Anna paused abruptly. There had been something in the gesture which brought her to a halt. It was a gesture which Hugh made quite often, but with herself. It was meant to convey that he cared about her, and now he was using that same gesture with Janet Fairbairn.

She saw Janet turning away and picking up a file of papers and her manner was quite brisk and business-like, but Anna stood outside for a long time.

Slowly she walked back down the path, glancing back to see that Janet was once again at her typewriter.

Back home Anna carefully removed the silk suit, then hung away Hugh's dark clothes. They would not be used that evening

*   *   *

Over the next few days Anna was too preoccupied with her own problem to worry about anything else. Mr Davidson had sent her a postcard asking her to call and collect her ring, and she found that the cost of the repair made a hole in her savings.

The ring now glowed with all the colours of the spectrum.

'It's a very fine stone indeed,' Mr Davidson confided. 'If you would like me to sell it for you — '

'No, thank you,' Anna interrupted hurriedly. 'It's not mine to sell.' She would have to ring Myra and ask her if the Stephen Fosters were home. It would have to be returned as soon as possible.

But even the ring was of small significance compared with her worries over her marriage. Every night Hugh was late home, claiming that he was having to travel further afield to find work for his firm. With misgivings she was being forced to acknowledge that they were beginning to drift apart.

She loved Hugh and the thought of losing him was causing her more heartache than she had ever known.

★   ★   ★

After Jill and Peter had both gone out one evening, Anna went slowly upstairs and into her bedroom. Sitting at her dressing-table, she studied her face in the mirror. There had been a time when Hugh had thought her beautiful and she had not changed so very much. Surely it must be possible for her to recapture his love if only she tried a little harder. It was not in her nature to give up easily.

Once again she laid out the pretty nightdress which old Mrs Foster had given her, and prepared herself for bed. Hugh didn't like her to wait up for him and she often read a book until he returned home. Tonight she could not relax and it seemed hours before her family arrived home and crept quietly up to bed.

Hugh opened their bedroom door softly then looked slightly disconcerted when he saw that Anna was still awake and the bedside light still threw a warm glow round the room.

'Hello, darling,' she said softly. 'I expect you're tired after such a long day.'

'Tired enough,' he admitted.

Swiftly she extinguished the light after Hugh had come to bed then, as she had done countless nights in the past, she began to talk to him about her day and to ponder on the affairs of their children.

'Jill seems to be enjoying Adrian Scott's company,' she said happily, then lay silent for a while, reflecting on her pleasure when Jill told her about the visit from old Dr Scott's grandson.

'How kind of the old man to think

about me, and to return the book,' she commented to Hugh. 'He's always been a true friend, he never believed that I neglected Mrs Foster. His defence of my character was one of the things that gave me comfort after the trial. It's a real shame he's not too well nowadays. I'd like to see him again,' she went on reflectively.

'And I would rather like to meet Elizabeth Caldwell,' she added. 'She must be special to have captured Peter's interest. He's never singled out any girls before. Hugh . . . Hugh?'

He grunted a little and she bit her lip. Was this, then, to be the pattern of their marriage. He could hardly stay awake long enough to talk to her for a little, even if it was only small, intimate family discussion precious only to a husband and wife?

How long was it since he had reached for her love, wondered Anna with an ache in her heart. How long was it since he had done more than kiss her cheek?

'Hugh?' she whispered, then slid her

arm over to touch him gently. It was as though she had burned him, and with a swift movement he turned away from her.

'Not now, Anna, I'm very tired,' he said and the warm heat of humiliation flooded over her, leaving her sick and shaken.

Elizabeth And Peter

The following morning, Anna was downstairs early, and as usual the family had little to say before they each went their separate ways.

Anna was glad, for once, to have the house to herself. She spent most of the morning clearing out the spare bedroom and moving in her personal belongings. She had no heart for making the room look particularly attractive, but she lifted her chin, determined to make the best of things as she found a pretty cover for the bed and small ornaments to put along the window ledge.

She also helped herself to a fluffy white rug from the bedroom she had shared with Hugh, and she was standing back, surveying her handiwork, when she heard a step at the bottom of the stairs and Hugh's voice called to her.

'Anna! Are you there?'

A moment later he had bounded upstairs. He was about to tell her something when he became aware of her morning's task and his eyes went wide with shock and disbelief.

'Just what do you think you're doing?' he asked harshly.

'You can see what I'm doing. I won't stay where I'm not wanted.'

Hugh's face was very white as Anna turned to face him. Even in the worst days during her trial and the aftermath, he had never seen such hurt and anger in her eyes.

'I don't understand . . . ' he began.

'Don't you, Hugh?' she asked quietly. 'There was a time when we could talk to one another, and perhaps even a time when we understood one another so well that there was no need for words. But we've lost that, Hugh. I don't think I need say any more.'

'Very well, you can have your own room since it means so much to you,' he said, his voice trembling with anger.

89

He stormed along the landing to their old bedroom and, a moment later, the door slammed between them. Anna put a hand up to her cheek. It was almost as though the door had hit her on the face.

She could hear the sounds of drawers being opened in his room, and the familiar creak of his wardrobe door, and knew that he was changing. She glanced at her watch, realising that it was lunch-time. Squaring her shoulders, she forced herself to accept the day as a normal one in her life. She was still a housewife and in charge of running the home.

Walking lightly down the stairs, she deposited the last few items of rubbish from the spare room into the dustbin and began to set the kitchen table.

The boiling kettle whistled piercingly, at exactly the same moment as the telephone rang and Hugh's bedroom door was thrown open. Anna dealt with the kettle, then picked up the telephone receiver, holding a hand over the mouthpiece as Hugh appeared at the kitchen door.

'Lunch is nearly ready, Hugh,' she said swiftly. 'I'll just see who's calling.'

'No need to hurry for me,' he returned, and she could see that he was still boiling with suppressed anger. 'I shall be eating out. I'll probably be late tonight, too.'

'That's nothing new,' she muttered. 'Hello?'

'Mrs Cameron?' The man's voice was deep and assured.

'This is Mrs Cameron speaking.'

'Stephen Foster here. My wife and I have just returned from London. I understand from our housekeeper that you called to see us . . . '

The front door slammed and Anna put a hand up to her forehead. Why did everything have to happen at once?

★ ★ ★

'Oh, hello, Mr Foster,' she said nervously, her voice sounding high and unnatural. 'Yes, I did call to see you. I — I wanted to return your grandmother's ring.'

'So you have got it!' Stephen Foster's voice was triumphant. 'I thought so,' he added. 'And you've decided to return it after I started making enquiries. That's very good of you, Mrs Cameron. I must say it is encouraging that you're turning over a new leaf.'

His voice was full of sarcasm and Anna's cheeks flushed scarlet. How dare he talk to her like this!

'I have only just discovered that the ring has any value, Mr Foster,' she said with quiet dignity. 'Your grandmother gave it to me — '

'I bet she did!'

'She gave it to me,' Anna insisted quietly, 'but I wouldn't dream of keeping it now that I know it's valuable. If you're at home now, Mr Foster, I'll bring it round to you straight away.'

Anna had to catch a bus to the Fosters' home and it was almost forty minutes before she reached the house.

Stephen Foster and his wife rose to their feet as Anna was shown into the room.

The box was still in the envelope stamped with Davidson the jeweller's name and address, and she handed the whole thing over to Mr Foster after a brief greeting to both of them.

'The ring had to be reset, Mr Foster,' she explained. 'The centre stone was loose. Mrs Foster — your grandmother — advised me to have it done. It was only then that I learned that the stone was a diamond. I had thought it might be a spinel or even a white zircon.'

'I'm sure you did,' Mr Foster said heavily. 'You say that my grandmother gave it to you without telling you it was a diamond?'

'She did.'

'Yet apparently you know enough about jewellery to decide that it must be a spinel or a zircon. Surely it requires knowledge to know that these stones can resemble diamonds, so I find it hard to believe that you didn't know my grandmother's ring was a very fine diamond solitaire.'

He was holding it out and the ring sparkled with light in its new setting.

'It certainly looks like a diamond now,' she said calmly. 'Mr Davidson has cleaned and repaired it. Since you are familiar with it, Mr Foster, I have no doubt that you remember that the setting was poor and the stone had become dulled . . . '

'A diamond lasts for ever, Mrs Cameron.'

She drew herself up with quiet dignity.

'I can only repeat, Mr Foster, that I had no intention of keeping the ring as soon as I learned its value, even though it was a gift. I would have returned it immediately but you were away. Now I can only be thankful to see it in your hands. Good afternoon, Mr Foster, Mrs Foster, I'm sure I can see myself out.'

She turned to go but not before she saw a look of uncertainty on Stephen Foster's face.

★ ★ ★

That evening Anna prepared a dinner for Peter, Jill and herself. For once her children were spending an evening at home, with Jill declaring that she had to wash her hair and Peter asking to borrow Anna's old portable typewriter to answer a few letters.

Anna had walked most of the way home from the Fosters' and the fresh air had revived her and had given her a better appetite.

Jill had been perplexed to find that her tennis racket and lacrosse stick now occupied a corner of her own room.

'I put them there,' her mother explained, the colour rising slightly in her cheeks. 'Your camera equipment, Peter, is now in a box on top of your wardrobe, too. I've cleaned out the spare bedroom.' She tried to speak casually.

'Why?' Jill's eyes were puzzled. 'Is Aunt Helen coming?' she asked. 'It's ages since she's been here and she's always a lot of fun . . . '

'And a soft touch,' Peter added. 'She spoiled us and she's still spoiling Jill. Just look at her eyes lighting up at the prospect.'

'You're a fine one to talk!' Jill cried indignantly. 'You're always getting round Aunt Helen. I love her for herself.'

'Be quiet, both of you,' Anna said, so sharply that the teasing stopped and Jill and Peter turned round at once to stare at her.

'Aunt Helen is not coming,' she went on. 'In her last letter she said she was going on a cruise to the Greek Islands or somewhere. The spare bedroom is for me. It's mine now. I — I just feel I would like my own room for a while. I don't sleep very well these nights and — and I don't want to disturb your father.'

She wasn't good at lying to her children. Her cheeks were now highly coloured and she was well aware of the significant looks being exchanged behind her back.

After supper, Anna excused herself, deciding to go to bed early. Mention of her aunt, Miss Helen Aitken, had reminded her that she hadn't replied to the older woman's last letter. Anna sighed. If only Aunt Helen lived nearer to Castleden, how comforting it would be.

But Anna's parents and grandparents had belonged to Ayrshire and Aunt Helen, who was now her only relative, still lived in Ayr.

Anna rested her aching head on her pillow. Not even with her broadminded, well-balanced aunt could she talk over her present problems. Her last thought, before she dropped into an exhausted sleep, was that it had been a long day. She didn't hear Hugh returning home only a few minutes before midnight.

When Anna had moved into her own bedroom, she had been following the dictates of her heart and the need to preserve her independence. It hadn't occurred to her that the price of independence must be paid for each day, as well as during the lonely nights. Her desertion of Hugh had angered him so that he had withdrawn behind a wall of reserve which threatened to cut him off from the whole family. It was a difficult situation.

Hugh brooded heavily and decided he would be as little trouble to Anna as possible. It was easy enough for him to have a sandwich out at lunch-time, and if he and Janet worked late, they often shared a 'carry-out' meal in the office.

Jill was least affected by the strained atmosphere at home. Thanks to Adrian Scott, she was beginning to enjoy every day to the full once more.

So far, she and Adrian had sought quiet pursuits and had walked a great deal in the country. They had pursued old Dr Scott's archaeological interests in the evidence of local Roman occupation.

In this, Anna had also been able to help and she took a great delight in

Adrian's visits to their home. She had gone to see her old friend, Dr Scott, taking him a gift of his favourite home-made raspberry jam. It saddened her, though, that his health was now so poor.

★ ★ ★

'There's a concert on next Friday evening at the Civic Centre,' Adrian told Jill one day. 'Wouldn't you like to go to that for a change? It isn't too highbrow.'

Jill paused. Everything was going well at school now, but she had to steel herself to go out in public. Adrian said it was only her own imagination that made her believe people kept glancing at her.

'Come on, Jill. I don't know what you're hiding from anyway. Your mother is a wonderful woman. You should be proud of her.'

'I am proud of her,' Jill replied indignantly.

'Then stop hurting her by showing how much you mind people pointing their fingers. People who do that sort of thing usually have plenty in their own lives to cause them shame. Deep inside they're diverting attention from themselves. There you are — the lecture for the day. Let's go to the concert.'

'OK,' Jill said, then grinned. 'Thanks, Adrian.'

He leaned over and kissed her lightly.

'Think nothing of it,' he whispered.

The first part of the concert was devoted to works by Mendelssohn which were so popular that Jill was familiar with every note. She allowed her mind to wander and her thoughts kept turning again and again to her parents. Was she right in thinking that her father spent too much time away from home?

At the interval, Adrian escorted Jill out into the foyer for coffee.

'Well? Are you enjoying it?' he asked.

'Yes, very nice,' Jill said lamely. What would happen if her parents split up?

That would cause a great deal more talk. Besides, how could she bear such a thing . . . ?

Adrian was looking at her closely.

'No, you're not! You've been miles away. Is there anything wrong?'

'No, I'm fine,' she assured him hurriedly.

She almost had to shout as the noise built up round them, then there was a sudden lull and she could hear a woman's voice clearly behind her.

'Oh, look, isn't that Anna Cameron's daughter over there with the tall young man with fair hair?'

Jill's body began to burn with heat. She felt that dozens of pairs of eyes were upon her, boring into her back. Her new-found confidence began to drain away.

'I've got to go, Adrian,' she said urgently. 'I — I'm sorry. I just can't stay. Bye.'

Before he could even grab her arm, she had slipped through the crowds and out into the street. A bus was passing and Jill stepped aboard even as she caught sight of Adrian emerging from the doorway of the Civic Centre.

Her eyes were blinded by tears as she made her way home. She was still an object of curiosity to some people, but she would ensure that Adrian was not. No-one would whisper about him behind his back because of her, or her family.

* * *

It had been a pleasant evening for Elizabeth Caldwell. It was several months now since she had first met Peter Cameron, when he came to assess for fire damage at a local hostel.

Elizabeth's home was in Edinburgh, but she had been transferred as relief clerk to the Castleden branch of the bank for which she worked, and had taken a room at the hostel. Unfortunately, one of the girls in the hostel had left a chip pan on the stove and the kitchen walls had been badly blackened as a result.

Elizabeth had been present when Peter came to make his enquiries and they had got talking, then he had invited her to the sports club. After she returned to Edinburgh, she often thought about the tall, brown-haired young man with the thoughtful dark eyes.

When she was offered a permanent post in Castleden, Elizabeth hadn't hesitated. She liked the small town where everyone seemed to know everyone else. And everyone else's business . . .

At first she had been startled, and perhaps rather shocked, when one of her colleagues at the bank told her that Mrs Cameron had served a prison sentence.

★　★　★

Elizabeth had accepted Anna's invitation to supper, again with a hint of reserve, but that had vanished very

103

quickly after being welcomed into Peter's home by his mother.

Elizabeth had felt the warmth of Anna Cameron's personality as soon as she stepped over the doorstep. At the moment she rented a bed-sitting room near to the bank and she missed her parents and younger brother very much.

Now she had to fight back the tears as she was so warmly welcomed into Peter's home, and she saw how much his mother appreciated her visit. It was lovely to be in a real family atmosphere once more.

'You must promise to come again,' the older woman insisted when Elizabeth rose to leave. 'It must be lonely for you leaving your family and friends in Edinburgh. You mustn't feel lonely, my dear.'

Peter was working away from home for the early part of the following week, but when he called to see Elizabeth again, she was shocked to see that his frank open face looked thinner and his bright eyes were clouded with worry.

'Do you mind if we don't go out this evening?' he asked Elizabeth. 'Is it all right if we just sit and talk? I don't feel I want to concentrate on badminton this evening.'

'Do you want to go home and keep your mother company?' Elizabeth asked.

He shook his head.

'No, Jill's home at the moment. She and Adrian Scott seem to have had a tiff, but I doubt if it's serious.'

'I'll make us a cup of coffee in a moment,' Elizabeth offered. 'What do you want to talk about?'

'A person. A girl,' Peter said heavily.

'A girl?' Elizabeth echoed warily.

'A nurse. Sharon Bell. Does the name mean anything to you?'

'I can't say it does,' Elizabeth confessed.

'No, people forget girls like Sharon,' Peter said bitterly. 'She was only a witness at my mother's trial. She's been forgotten, but everyone in Castleden knows all about Anna Cameron.' He sighed.

'Everyone believed Sharon Bell's evidence,' he explained to Elizabeth. 'It was my mother who was made out to be a liar. Well, I don't believe it. I've thought about it and thought about it till I'm tired, and I just don't believe that girl's evidence. She said my mother never changed duties with her and didn't telephone her to ask her to come in early the day Mrs Foster died.'

'Isn't it better to let it rest now?' Elizabeth asked gently. 'Surely it's all over and done with.'

'It isn't over and done with,' Peter said. 'It's ruining my mother's life — my parents' marriage. It's even ruining Jill's life, and who knows what effect it may yet have on mine? And all because that nurse wouldn't tell the truth. I know one thing, Elizabeth, I won't rest until I've found her again, until I shake the truth out of her.'

Elizabeth felt a sudden stab of fear.

'No, Peter,' she whispered, 'let it

alone. You might only make things worse.'

'I can't make them any worse,' he said heavily. 'I tell you, Elizabeth, I've got to find her.'

Elizabeth sighed. Having made up his mind, Peter was unshakable. Perhaps that was one of the things she found attractive about him.

'Can I help?' she asked, and a smile lit up his face.

'I can't ask Mum for Sharon's address. I'll have to do it all behind her back. I know Sharon had a telephone, because Mum used to call her sometimes about changing shifts, despite the fact that Sharon claimed they never altered their hours.

'The trouble is, I don't think she lived at home. I think she had a flat somewhere and the number might be listed under her landlady's name. I'll try the telephone book first.' He smiled again. 'Have you seen how many people called Bell live in this area? How long have we got before your landlady throws me out?'

'Just over an hour.' Elizabeth laughed.

'Then help me find addresses and telephone numbers in Castleden. I can't telephone from here, I know, but I'll spend some time on it tomorrow.'

Peter began to read out names, addresses and telephone numbers, and Elizabeth painstakingly wrote down the numbers which showed promise.

'If those are no good, I'll keep going until I've telephoned all of them,' Peter vowed.

She looked at the new animation on his face. It was almost fanatical, and again she sighed inwardly. There would be no peace for Peter until he had found Sharon Bell.

It was late when he returned home.

Out Of The Blue

Anna could see that Hugh had a very special appointment when he came down to breakfast the following morning. She handed him the shoes which matched his suit, and checked up on his tie and socks. His hair was in a tuft again and she almost moved forward to brush it into place, but the barrier of pride and hurt was still between them.

'You're all dressed up, Hugh,' she remarked. 'Is it something special today?'

For a moment he was tempted to confide in her, then he choked back the words.

'It's — well — nothing special,' he said awkwardly. 'I have to go to Edinburgh, that's all.'

Anna's eyes darkened as she watched him go. He was lying to her. No, perhaps that was too strong. He was evading her questions and that, to her mind, was even worse. Surely he could still talk to her a little and tell her things of general interest. But it seemed to her that Hugh was deliberately shutting her out of his life.

Anna sighed as she tidied up the kitchen table and reminded both Jill and Peter that they should be downstairs by now. Peter was in a more cheerful mood as he ate his breakfast. He had been abstracted recently and Anna had watched him worriedly. Perhaps he and Elizabeth were at odds with one another over something. The matter must have been resolved, however, and now Peter was reasonably early for work.

'I have a few phone calls to make before I start,' he told her.

'Is Elizabeth OK, then?' she asked.

'Sure, she's fine,' Peter answered.

Anna nodded, satisfied. Peter's recent preoccupation was no doubt related to his work.

On the other hand it seemed to her

that Jill and Adrian Scott had hit a stumbling block in their friendship. Jill seemed very reluctant to keep dates with Adrian in the evenings, even though the telephone had been red-hot with his persistent calls.

It rang just as Jill was sitting down at the breakfast table, assuring her mother that she had no appetite for anything other than toast.

Anna picked up the receiver, then turned with a smile to Jill.

'It's Adrian again. He says it's important.'

Jill sighed and took the receiver.

'I seem to remember that we were going to Mellerstain on Saturday,' Adrian said cheerfully.

'I can't go. I've got exams coming up.'

'It'll do you good to get out,' Adrian reasoned.

'Tell me that after I've failed,' Jill retorted.

'You won't fail. I'll ask you questions on your paper as we walk about. It's the best way to study.'

'But, Adrian — ' Jill found herself weakening.

'I'll look in this evening and you can think about it,' he interrupted.

'No, Adrian!'

But the line had gone dead and Jill looked at her mother with exasperation. She sighed.

'Doesn't Adrian Scott ever take no for an answer?'

'Not if he's like his grandfather.' Anna laughed. 'If old Dr Scott couldn't find an answer to a problem over a patient, he used to dig and dig into all his medical books. Adrian's rather like him.'

The telephone shrilled again and Jill picked it up.

'I've told you, Adrian,' she began, then her voice faltered. 'Oh, I'm sorry . . . Yes, she's here now.' She turned to her mother. 'For you, Mum. It's Janet Fairbairn.'

Anna's eyes grew cool. What could Janet Fairbairn want?

'Yes, Miss Fairbairn?' she asked politely.

Janet heard the note of constraint in Anna Cameron's voice and she felt rather taken aback.

'It . . . it's about Hugh, Mrs Cameron,' she said. 'I only wondered if he was calling here at the office. There's a rather urgent telephone call for him.'

'I'm sorry I can't help you, Miss Fairbairn,' said Anna quietly. 'I don't know his plans.'

There was a tiny silence.

'I . . . I see,' Janet said. 'I think I can deal with it. I'm sorry to have troubled you.'

Janet put down the receiver with troubled eyes. She hadn't failed to recognise the cool note in Anna Cameron's voice. It was easy to guess that all wasn't well between Hugh and his wife.

★　★　★

Hugh returned in the late afternoon, his eyes again a little tired.

113

'Have you had lunch?' Janet asked.

'We had a business lunch, but I didn't eat much,' Hugh said. 'I hadn't much appetite.'

She handed him a mug of coffee and rustled up a cheese sandwich.

'Then you didn't call in at home on the way here?'

Hugh's eyes flickered.

'No. Why? There isn't anything wrong, is there?'

Janet paused. Hugh's relationship with his wife was really none of her business except — except that she had grown to respect and admire him as they worked closely together, and above everything else, she wanted him to be happy. It hurt her to see the sudden hint of pain in his eyes whenever she mentioned his wife, or his home.

'I tried to reach you at home, but you had gone. Johnstone's rang and wanted to speak to you urgently. But it turned out they only wanted the estimate for repairs and not rebuilding. I managed to deal with it,' she told him.

'Fine,' Hugh told her.

'But when I spoke to your wife, she sounded so odd, Hugh. I — I've been a bit worried all day. I hope it isn't anything I've done, or said, even . . . '

There was an awkward silence between them, then Hugh reached over and took her hand.

'It's nice of you to be concerned about us, Janet. I'm grateful for that. In fact, you've no idea how grateful I feel just to have someone I can talk to . . . Oh, all right, you'd better know. Things aren't awfully good between Anna and me. In fact, she's moved out of our bedroom and into a room of her own.'

'Oh, Hugh!' Janet was shocked but her voice was full of ready sympathy.

'Oh, it was probably my fault,' Hugh went on, 'though I'm not taking all the blame. It all goes back to Mrs Foster. As Myra says, Anna should really have thought things out a little more when she left the old lady that day. We all know she didn't deliberately neglect her, but she was careless in doing her job.

'I think she forgot about everything in worrying over Jill, and she just rushed home. The old woman paid with her life, Anna paid with a prison sentence and now all of us are paying, day after day. It's hard to see work slipping away . . . '

'It'll soon be forgotten, Hugh. You've just got to weather it. Massey's won't care about your private life. They're a big concern, not like some around here with their narrow minds.'

'I know, but it's all the little things which count, Janet. They wear me out. We've seen it, haven't we, my dear? But Anna hasn't, or maybe not quite so much. She just works in the house. She's not in business, struggling to make a living.'

He grew quiet and she knew that there was a deep-rooted feeling of insecurity in him, and a fear of failure. She knew very well what he was going through.

'I think you'll have to make the effort to heal the breach, Hugh,' she said at length.

'Make the effort?' Hugh echoed. 'What do you mean? You don't know Anna when you say things like that.'

'Oh yes, I do. She's a gentle, sensitive woman and she'll be aching for you to make the first move towards her. Why don't you arrange a wee holiday somewhere?'

'I can't afford it,' Hugh said flatly.

'Can you afford to lose your life's happiness, Hugh? Don't you want Anna's love back again?'

Hope began to rise in him. He had missed Anna very much. He had missed the relationship which had once bound them so closely together, and the happy family atmosphere in which he could relax and forget all other troubles. He had missed Anna's soothing hands and gentle love, and the small precious moments which only a husband and wife could enjoy.

'If you can't afford Paris, then make

it Scarborough or Blackpool.' Janet laughed. She could see that she was convincing him.

'I'll see what Anna says,' he told her. He dropped a kiss lightly on to the top of her hair. 'Thanks, Janet.'

'All in the service.' She smiled, then turned away to hide the sudden rush of tears to her eyes. She had her own secret feelings, but they belonged to her alone. She had no claim on anyone else's love.

* * *

It was proving a long day for Anna. She had been upset over Hugh's attitude to her that morning, but she put it to the back of her mind when the post arrived.

There was a chatty letter from her Aunt Helen in Ayr.

It was a very quick reply to her own letter and the contents brought the warmth of excitement to Anna's cheeks.

She could hardly wait for her family

to return home that evening in order to discuss the letter, but as it was, she was doomed to disappointment. Both Jill and Peter wanted their meal postponed.

Adrian Scott had called to see Jill and he met her at the gate as she returned home. They were arguing together as Jill opened the front door with her key and led Adrian into the sitting-room.

'I've told you, Adrian, I just can't spare the time.'

'You can't afford not to spare the time, Jill. All work and no play, etc.,' Adrian argued. 'I can't imagine that Jill would ever be a dull girl, but she is a bit droopy. Come on, Jill, we'll go for a walk along the riverbank, and make plans for Mellerstain on Saturday.'

In spite of herself, Jill's eyes crinkled at Adrian's cajoling tone.

'Mum's got tea ready,' she said.

'And you're invited, Adrian,' Anna said, smiling happily as she looked into the sitting-room.

'Oh dear, I'm so sorry, Mrs Cameron, but I don't think I can stay,'

Adrian sad. 'My grandfather expects me home in a little while. You know I live with him since my mother died and my father is away so much. I only came to persuade Jill to go for a walk with me so that we can make plans for Saturday . . . '

Adrian looked so crestfallen that Anna laughed heartily.

'Make it Saturday evening then,' she said, then her eyes grew thoughtful as she remembered something. 'At least . . . Never mind, Adrian, Jill will arrange something. I'm sure.'

'He's an awful bully,' Jill said. 'He takes no notice of my wishes.'

'Come on. We'll give your mother a chance to finish her cooking.'

Anna watched them go, her heart warmed by the sight of their companionship. Adrian Scott was determined to be a steadfast friend to Jill. She saw Peter arriving and for a short while he talked earnestly to the other two, then he rushed indoors.

'Can you hold up making tea for Jill

and me for a little while, Mum?' he asked. 'We're just going home with Adrian. He has . . . er . . . something I'd like to borrow.'

Anna sighed. Once again her family were deserting her. It was too much to expect that Hugh would arrive home early, and that they could have tea together. In any case she was in no mood for one of his long silences.

She watched Jill and Peter getting into Adrian's old car which roared away with a great deal of noise.

'You're sure your grandfather won't mind talking to me?' Peter asked rather anxiously as he sat beside Adrian in the front of the car.

'No, of course not,' Adrian replied confidently. 'He's happy to find all the time in the world for the Camerons. It really upset him about what happened to your mother. If only he hadn't been feeling off colour at the time, I think he would have been out in the streets holding a banner to proclaim a miscarriage of justice.'

'What do you want to see Dr Scott about, anyway?' Jill asked her brother.

'I want to find Sharon Bell.'

'Sharon Bell?' Jill's voice rose. 'Not that girl again! Oh, Peter, for goodness' sake, leave it alone. Haven't we suffered enough?'

'That's just it,' Peter said heatedly. 'We've suffered enough. Haven't you realised what a difference it might make if we found out the girl had been telling lies at the trial?'

'But it's all over now,' Jill argued despairingly. 'Old Mrs Foster's dead and nothing can put that right. That's how Mum feels, too. She won't want you to rake things over.'

'But Mum's still being blamed for it, even by members of her own family. Oh, yes, she is, Jill, even by you and me.'

'Not you, Peter. You never blamed her.'

'Perhaps, at times, I did. We all did. Have you listened to our Myra's snide remarks? And don't you think that she and Dad — ' Peter broke off, colouring furiously.

He had forgotten that Adrian Scott was not a member of the family. Jill was glaring warnings at him with heightened colour in her cheeks.

'Dad stuck by Mum through thick and thin,' she said loudly.

'Of course he did. But Mum isn't happy. She's far too bright at times. Adrian must know what I mean.'

'Perhaps I do,' Adrian said slowly. 'She wants to show everyone how normal her life is now, but she goes over the top. I think Peter's right, Jill. It might make a big difference to your mother if he found out that the nurse was lying. My grandfather always wondered about that, though he admitted he had nothing against the girl. It was generally accepted that she was a nice girl.'

'That's right,' Peter said. 'Mum thought so, too. That's why she was so upset and wouldn't insist too loudly that Sharon was lying. Mum was fond of her. Instead she used to keep worrying that *she* might have been the one to make a mistake and hadn't made the arrangements she thought she had with Sharon.

'Somehow their lines had become crossed. She knew the girl was lying, though, when she said she never had swapped duties with Mum. I mean, I know that. I heard Mum making just such an arrangement on the telephone once. I know there's no doubt of that.'

'Then why didn't you give evidence?'

'Because I couldn't hear what Sharon was saying. I only had Mum's word for it, but I'd back her against Sharon with my dying breath.'

*   *   *

Old Dr Scott looked frail and his movements were made painful by arthritis, but his eyes brightened when he heard Peter's request and shrewdly demanded to know the reason for it.

'So you're going to find that young woman and have a good talk to her, are you?' he asked. 'Now you're showing some sense, my boy.' He took a file from his desk.

'This was Sharon's address when she was Mrs Foster's nurse,' he said, giving Peter a slip of paper. 'I don't know whether or not she's still there. It's a house that was turned into bed-sitting rooms and it's mainly used by nurses.'

'It's a start,' Peter said. 'Thanks, Doctor Scott.'

'Don't forget to let me know how you get on,' the old man said.

'I won't,' Peter promised.

It was half an hour later before Jill and Peter returned home. Anna had sat down and helped herself to some of the chicken casserole which was still keeping hot in the oven. She had waited long enough for her family, she thought rather crossly, but the long wait had settled something in her mind.

They could well do without her over the next month. With a bit of planning she could leave her home so that none of them were inconvenienced.

She got out her letter which had arrived that morning from Aunt Helen, and read it yet again.

I'm so disappointed, Helen Aitken had written in her large, spidery hand. *At least, I was until I thought about you, Anna dear.*

Sarah McIntosh and I had arranged a trip to the Greek islands, but Sarah has had to cancel. She's been waiting nearly two years for a minor operation and now her name has come up. At such a time, too! But she says she'll go to the back of the queue if she doesn't get it attended to, and she'll have another chance to go to the Greek islands, this time feeling one hundred per cent.

I suppose she's being sensible, but it leaves me without a companion and although I consider myself young and spry, I sometimes get reminders that I'm over seventy now!

When your letter arrived, I thought about you, my dear.

The snag is that I can't give you long to consider. We would have to leave on

Friday. We could meet in Carlisle at an appointed time, dear. Could you telephone me on Thursday morning, about nine o'clock? I'll stay by my telephone and wait for your call. I would have called you but I thought you'd like a little time to think it over.

Anna decided that she needed no time at all, but when her children arrived home, she was not so sure. They were bickering, as usual, but she could feel the love they had to offer her as soon as they walked in the door.

She told them about the holiday.

'Wow, Mum! Are you really going to go?' Their eyes were wide as they turned to look at her.

'What's all the excitement?' Hugh asked behind them. He had let himself quietly into the house.

'It's Mum,' Jill explained. 'She's going to the Greek islands with Aunt Helen. On Friday. Isn't it exciting?'

Over Jill's head Anna turned and met Hugh's startled gaze.

'I Must Be Fair'

'I've had to decide in a hurry, Hugh,' Anna said quietly. 'The holiday's already booked and I'm just taking someone else's place. But — if you feel I ought not to go. I mean, if it's going to mean a lot of inconvenience for you while I'm away, then of course I won't dream of going.'

Angrily he turned away from her.

'Why consult me?' he asked, his voice tightly controlled. 'You can do what you like, of course. I've managed very well without you before now, and I can manage again.'

Anna's head went down and she bit her lip. Once again she felt as though Hugh had slammed a door in her face. She should have known better than to ask him about anything.

Hugh had turned away and was once again making for the stairs, his face hard and set.

Jill had been too excited by the thought of going through her own things and finding useful items for her mother to take with her to see anything unusual between her parents.

But Peter could hardly speak for the sickness in his heart. Couldn't his parents see how much they were hurting one another?

Peter's mouth firmed as he thought about the events which had led up to their present situation. Somehow he must find that nurse whose evidence had done so much harm to his mother.

He hesitated over placing an arm round his mother's shoulders to comfort her, then decided against it. She was at great pains to hide her hurt feelings. He must pretend that all was well.

The following morning Hugh left early for the office after a hurried breakfast.

Her head ached and Anna had never felt less like preparing for a holiday, but she rose quickly and splashed cold water on her face. She had now accepted Aunt Helen's invitation and she would put her mind towards helping her aunt to enjoy herself. Hugh must not be allowed to spoil that. If he didn't want her any more, she would have to learn to accept it.

Peter had left a message to say that he would not be home until later than usual.

'I suppose he's working late,' Anna said.

Jill turned away, saying nothing.

Peter's hopes were high as he rang the bell of the block of flats at the address given to him by Dr Scott. After a time a rather vague-looking woman, with wispy hair, came to open the door.

'We have no vacancies,' she said, 'and I only accommodate girls.'

'I don't want a flat,' he assured her. 'In fact, I've come to enquire about one of the girls who lives here — a nurse.'

'I'm afraid I don't answer questions about my tenants,' she said coldly. 'If you care to leave a letter, I'll put it on the rack.'

'I only want to know if she still lives here,' Peter said swiftly. 'Her name's Sharon Bell. I'm . . . I'm an old friend.'

'I see. That's a bit different. I can't help you, though. Nurse Bell isn't here now. She left to get married. She and her new husband were planning to rent a bigger flat.'

'Can you tell me where, and her married name?' Peter asked eagerly.

The woman shook her head. 'I don't know about the name, but I have an address somewhere — she gave me it for forwarding mail, but it'll take me a while to find it. Could you come back at the weekend, Mr . . . '

'Cameron. Peter Cameron,' he supplied.

The woman's eyes flickered, but again she nodded.

'I'll try to find it by Saturday afternoon, Mr Cameron.'

When Peter arrived home, Jill was still helping her mother with the last of her packing, but Hugh had not returned from the office. He had gone straight there after a long, tiring day, though his briefcase bulged with facts and figures which would have to be typed out by Janet Fairbairn.

★   ★   ★

Janet was still entering up the last of the monthly accounts and she looked up as he walked in the door.

'I've got a few urgent letters to be signed, Hugh,' she said.

'OK,' he said wearily. 'Leave them. You can go home when you're ready, Janet, but I'll work here for a little while.'

She stared at him uncertainly. 'Have you been home, Hugh? You look tired. Shall I make you a cup of coffee?'

'Please. No, I haven't been home yet.'

Something in his voice alerted her and her eyes grew solemn as she returned to his desk with the steaming hot cup of coffee.

'What happened about the holiday?'

she asked quietly.

'What holiday?' He smiled rather bitterly. 'The one you thought I ought to have with Anna, or the one she has arranged with her Aunt Helen? She leaves in the morning for the start of a trip to the Greek islands.'

Janet's eyes widened. 'You — you mean she preferred to go with her aunt rather than go away for a holiday with you?'

'No, it wasn't quite like that, Janet.' Hugh sighed. 'I must be fair. I went home intending to ask Anna about a holiday, but I found that the other one was already arranged. So that was that.'

'I see,' Janet said.

Janet looked at Hugh, noting the grim twist to his mouth and the faint lines at the sides of his eyes. His hair was standing up in tufts and she longed to smooth it down and to put her arms round him and soothe the tight worried lines from his forehead, but she had no right even to touch him.

'It's getting late, Janet.' Hugh's voice

broke into her thoughts. 'Better cut along home now. We'll leave all this for another day.'

'All right, Hugh. Good night,' she said.

'Night, Janet.'

Quietly she let herself out of the office.

★   ★   ★

Anna was meeting her Aunt Helen at a hotel in Carlisle before they boarded the train for London. It was not a long journey by car and she deliberated for some time, then decided to ask Hugh if he would take her to Carlisle.

If only they could be together for a little while, even in the car, perhaps they could talk and reach some sort of understanding of one another's problems.

Hugh looked tired when he arrived home. In spite of what he had said, he was not looking forward to the next three weeks when they would all return once again to an empty house each evening.

Jill's high, sweet voice mingled with Anna's lower-pitched tones in light bubbling laughter as Hugh pushed open the door, and his sense of grievance was once again outraged. He went straight into the kitchen, where his place was still set at the table, and fetched his meal from the oven.

He was still eating a piece of delicious cheesecake when Anna hurried downstairs.

'Oh, there you are, Hugh,' she said, brightly. In her nervousness, her voice was very light. 'Er ... I was wondering if you would be too busy to drive me to Carlisle to meet Aunt Helen ... '

Hugh poured himself another cup of tea and stirred it deliberately to control his anger. Was that all he meant in her life? She only wanted him when he was some use to her. Now he was being asked to chauffeur her to Carlisle!

'I'm sorry,' he said tonelessly. 'You

must surely know I can't spare the time.'

Anna's cheeks whitened, not at the refusal but at the tone. Hugh sounded as though he positively disliked her.

'I see,' she said quietly. 'I quite understand.'

'It's OK, Mum, Adrian and I can take you,' said Jill. 'Peter says he wants to come, too.'

'That's very nice of you all,' Anna said huskily. 'I'm most grateful.'

'Have you told Myra you're going?' Hugh asked suddenly.

'Yes,' Anna replied.

'What did she say?'

'She was delighted, of course,' Anna answered.

Myra had been more than delighted, Anna thought, tightly. It was not hard to fathom that her eldest daughter found her departure from Castleden a bit of a relief, even if it was only for a few short weeks. Besides, it was nice for her to be able to say to her friends . . . should they inquire . . . that her mother was on a cruise in the Greek islands.

Anna no longer had any illusions about Myra . . .

She looked at Hugh. He had risen to say he was going round to Myra's for a while, and she made no reply. Myra bitterly resented the fact that her mother had been in prison and it seemed that Hugh was beginning to accept her ideas as his own.

Anna's lips set in a straight line. She would go on this holiday with Aunt Helen, and she would try to forget everything else for the time being. After that, however, she would have to think very deeply about the future.

* * *

The sun shone the following day when Anna left her home to drive to Carlisle for the start of her exciting holiday.

That morning, Hugh had hesitated as she waited with quiet dignity whilst he picked up his belongings. Then he

137

turned to her and kissed her cheek.

'Have a good holiday, Anna.'

'Thank you, Hugh,' she replied coolly.

Her eyes were suddenly blinded by tears and she longed to feel his arms round her, but he quickly picked up his briefcase and made for the door. Sadly she watched him go.

They set off in plenty time, deciding not to take the main roads but stick to a quieter route. Anna was thoughtful as she stared out at the soft, beautiful countryside. What would she do if she had to make a new start in life? Where would she go?

How could she continue to live in Castleden if her marriage with Hugh broke up, and risk seeing him each day, knowing that they no longer belonged together?

In spite of the anticipation of the holiday, and the refreshing scenery, Anna's thoughts had tied themselves into tight knots when they eventually drove into Carlisle and parked in the hotel car park.

Aunt Helen had invited them all to have lunch with her in the hotel, and Jill could hardly sit still for excitement.

The youngster was first to greet her great-aunt in the foyer of the hotel, followed by Peter. Then Adrian Scott was introduced to the elderly lady and found himself meeting the clear searching gaze of the same clear eyes which he had come to associate with Jill and her mother.

Anna was bringing up the rear and for a small moment as her aunt reached out to hug her, she forgot to wear the bright mask she showed to the world, and Helen Aitken recoiled a little with shock.

Could this thin, rather intense woman be her beautiful Anna? She had gone to see Anna as often as she could while she was at Poplar Lodge and had been amazed at how well Anna was coping with her sentence.

But what had happened since? Anna was a deeply troubled woman, and for a moment Aunt Helen had misgivings.

Should they be going so far away when Anna felt like this? How would she cope with such a journey?

Helen Aitken felt frail and rather vulnerable. It was frustrating to be growing old and still have a young, adventurous heart in a body full of stiff old bones.

'I warn you I'm creaking in every joint,' she said to Anna. 'It's very good of you to come with an old crock like me, my dear.'

'Oh, Aunt Helen!' Anna exclaimed shakily. 'I think we both need this holiday.'

★　★　★

'What time's your date with Adrian?' Peter asked Jill the following morning.

'He'll be here soon,' she replied. 'We'll be away all day. Why do you want to know?'

'Oh . . . just interested,' Peter said vaguely.

He was due to go back and see Sharon Bell's previous landlady to obtain her new address in the early afternoon and he had been forced to break a date with Elizabeth in order to do so.

They had been going to spend the afternoon playing tennis, then on to a summer dance in the evening, but his new arrangements had forced Peter to alter his plans.

He had had no doubts that Elizabeth would understand and might even accompany him on the first part of his errand, which was to obtain the new address. After which, Peter had vague notions about picking her up later in the evening, after he had seen Sharon Bell, and they could still go to the dance.

But Elizabeth hadn't seen things that way . . .

'I'm sorry, Peter,' she said quietly, 'but I still want to play tennis.'

'Without a partner?'

'Oh, I'll still have a partner. There's sure to be somebody. In any case, you seem to forget I've got girlfriends as well as boyfriends who like a game. I shall go along as usual.'

'Then I'll call for you in the evening.'

'I can't promise to be here,' she demurred. 'Your arrangements could so easily be changed again, and I don't want to wait in all evening on my own. If everyone is going on somewhere, I shall go, too.'

'Aren't you being a wee bit huffy?' Peter asked, feeling rather huffy himself. 'I'm sorry I have to break dates, but you know the reason why and it's only a matter of rearrangement.'

A glint came into Elizabeth's eyes. She knew very well what Peter was trying to do, and she sympathised. Nevertheless, she was getting a little tired of being pushed into second place. He must learn that he could not just take her for granted.

'I'm not at all huffy,' she said pleasantly. 'What an idea! Just come along to the dance when you're free, Peter. I might be there, I might not.'

She smiled and he had to accept her

decision which, when he thought about it, was the most sensible thing from Elizabeth's point of view. Nevertheless, he could not help feeling put out.

But as the time drew near for Peter to call and collect Sharon Bell's new address, he forgot everything else in a wave of excitement.

'I don't know her new name,' the landlady repeated, 'because she was still unmarried when she moved to the other flat. I used to send any letters to Nurse Bell, as usual. But here is her new address.'

It was a block of larger flats on the other side of the town. The building was red sandstone and had been well cared for over the years. There were flower beds and well-cut grass surrounding the area, and Peter saw that the names of the flat-dwellers had been put up near the door. He would have to ask if anyone knew Sharon's new name, but suddenly his eyes were riveted on one of the names . . . Miss Sharon Bell.

She had not married after all! Or

perhaps no-one had bothered to alter the name.

He rang the bell, then climbed the stairs to the door of the flat, but there was no reply and he knocked again on the door, then listened carefully. There was no sound at all and Peter was forced to acknowledge, rather disconsolately, that the flat was empty and he must return later.

As he turned away he heard the lightness of a woman's step on the stairs and turned as she appeared on the landing.

'Nurse Bell?' he asked.

'Yes.'

'I'm Peter Cameron,' he said firmly. 'Anna Cameron's son.'

She drew in her breath sharply and he saw fear and apprehension in her eyes as she swiftly turned away from him.

'I'm very busy, Mr Cameron. I can't see anyone at the moment.'

'I would appreciate it if you would give me a few minutes of your time.'

* * *

Nurse Bell was blinking rapidly with agitation as she reached the door of her flat and stood with her back against it. It was like part of a nightmare coming true.

For months, ever since the trial, she'd dreaded meeting Anna Cameron again, or any member of her family.

It made her sick to think what had happened to Anna, and her own part in the affair. She couldn't talk about it to anyone.

'I'm afraid it's not at all convenient to see anyone just now. I can't imagine why you want to see me, in any case.'

Peter stood firmly beside her.

'I could explain better if we both sat down for a moment, and I assure you I won't take up more of your time than is absolutely necessary. I've come to see you because of my mother. She's deeply unhappy, and if you ever had any regard for her in the past — and I believe you did — then perhaps you will listen to me now.'

Sharon Bell raised her hands to her ears. 'I don't want to hear. I don't have to listen. You don't realise that — that your mother's trial was a bad time for me as well as for her. I — I just don't want to dwell on it any more. It's all in the past as far as I'm concerned,' she told him, her voice shrill and jagged.

Peter looked at her reflectively, noticing the signs of strain in her. Perhaps it would be better to leave her now, give her time to get used to the fact that he had found her.

'It might do you good to talk a little,' he said in a gentler voice. 'Think about it until I come back to see you again.'

'I don't want you to come back and see me. I have nothing to say to you.'

'Nevertheless, you'll have to get used to my knocking on your door,' Peter said pleasantly. 'I intend to call again and again, until you decide that you might as well answer a few questions.'

'Please go!' she cried. 'If you don't, I shall call — '

'The police?' Peter interjected. 'I

don't think that will be necessary. I merely wish to talk to you as a friend of my mother's. She was always very fond of you, you know.' He turned away and ran lightly down the stairs.

Sharon Bell could scarcely fit her key into the lock on the door. Then the door flew open so that she stumbled inside. Her legs were trembling and she was forced to sit down.

From the wide windows of her flat, she could see Peter Cameron's tall figure as he crossed the street and made his way towards the bus stop. What did he want with her? Why couldn't he leave her alone? She wanted to forget all about Anna Cameron's trial and the death of old Mrs Foster, but now it seemed that Peter Cameron was going to force her to re-live it all over again.

More Than A Friend

Peter was thoughtful as he travelled home on the bus. He didn't feel very much like dressing up to go dancing, but he felt the need to see Elizabeth and to talk to her for a little while.

She was dancing with another man when he arrived at the social club where they all met on a Saturday evening. He stood on the fringe of the crowd while the music resounded throughout the hall, and watched her as she danced to the music. She was smiling at something her partner had said, and her eyes sparkled happily.

Why should he try to gain Elizabeth's attention, he asked himself, bleakly. There was no reason why she should listen to his troubles.

He was making for the door when he heard Elizabeth's voice behind him. 'Peter! Peter, wait a moment!'

Elizabeth had danced for most of the evening, but it had not been the same without Peter.

'Peter!' she called again, and he turned to her thankfully.

'Hello, Elizabeth.'

'You were leaving,' she said accusingly.

'I know. I'm not good company for anybody tonight. You would have a much better time without me.'

'I've had as much dancing as I want,' she assured him. 'It was hot and stuffy in there. Can't we go for a walk? Let's take the path along the river bank. My feet are aching and the grass is nice and springy.' She took his arm. 'What's wrong, Peter? Didn't you find Nurse Bell after all?'

Peter was silent for a moment as they walked along together.

'Yes. I found her all right, but . . . but I keep having doubts now about what I'm doing, yet I know deep down that I must keep on at her.'

'What do you mean, Peter?'

'She wouldn't talk to me. I tried to insist, but she wouldn't even allow me into the flat.'

'Perhaps her husband was in,' Elizabeth suggested.

'She hasn't married.'

'Boyfriend, then. Perhaps . . . well, you know . . . she didn't want you to see him.'

'No, it wasn't that.' Peter shook his head slowly. 'The flat was empty, I feel sure of that. I think she was frightened, Elizabeth. She didn't want me to start asking awkward questions.'

'You . . . you didn't intimidate her, did you, Peter?' Elizabeth looked up at him.

'Of course not,' he denied. 'At least, I don't think so. I just made it clear that I was determined to have it out with her. But, later, I kept seeing her face, and I know she's an unhappy girl, Elizabeth. Perhaps she has enough troubles of her own. But if you want my opinion, the troubles all stem from the same source as ours. I think she lied at the trial, and her conscience isn't easy.'

'Don't you think she might be unhappy because her marriage hasn't taken place?' she suggested.

'Perhaps.' Peter pursed his lips.

The sky had darkened into twilight, and there was a dewy wetness on the grass beneath their feet. The low murmur of the river was soothing, as were the plaintive calls of night birds. Long fingers of scarlet had begun to shoot across the sky from the west, and Peter breathed deeply on the night air.

Elizabeth began to pull on her heavy white cardigan and Peter held the sleeves for her. His arm remained round her shoulders and he drew her into his arms. His hand reached out to caress her cheek, and he bent to kiss her, a warm, sweet, loving kiss.

Elizabeth's heart raced. She was growing very fond of Peter Cameron, but had doubts about his feelings for her. Perhaps he wanted to hold her close because he needed comfort rather than because he desired her.

'It's getting chilly,' she said gently. 'Perhaps we ought to go home, Peter.'

He looked down at her sweet face. Again he asked himself if he had the right to involve her in his affairs. Was he really entitled to hold up his head proudly and be a worthwhile friend for this girl? Would it not be better for her to form friendships with other men whose families had never been involved in even a breath of scandal?

'It's better that I take you home,' he said almost roughly.

* * *

On Monday morning Jill looked at the remains of the breakfast dishes, and the large pile of washing which had accumulated, and began to throw some of it into the washing machine.

It had been agreed that, since she was on holiday now, she would deal with the day-to-day housework.

Hugh began to grow used to Anna's being away once more, though he missed the smooth running of the household. Returning home one evening, he discovered that Jill had had a bit of a disaster when she was washing his underwear.

'What happened, Jill?' he asked.

'One of your maroon socks got into the washing machine by mistake,' she apologised. 'I tried to wash everything white again from pink, but the colour has stayed fast.'

'I prefer not to have pink underwear, Jill,' her father said.

'It was a sheer accident, Daddy!' she cried. 'It's easy to make a mistake when there's a lot of washing and . . . and ironing to be done.'

'Don't upset yourself, dear,' Hugh said. 'I can soon have it attended to. Why not send things to the laundry if it's too much for you?'

'Mum managed with time to spare,' Jill said miserably. 'Why can't I do the same?' —

Hugh sighed as Jill went back downstairs, then fetched a carrier bag.

When Anna had been away at Poplar Lodge he often took his laundry to Janet. She even sewed on buttons and mended any small holes. Perhaps she would know how to bleach this lot white again.

Hugh breezed into the office rather later than usual the following morning and found Janet working steadily at her typewriter.

'There are a few more estimates in from suppliers for the materials on the supermarket job, Hugh,' she said. 'That means doing a bit more costing if you can spare the time.'

Hugh shook his head as he picked up the morning's mail.

'Not till later on, Janet,' he said. 'We can't neglect ordinary jobs, in case we don't land this one. I must look at that household job in King Street.' He smiled suddenly.

'Oh, by the way, I've brought a bag of my laundry, if that's OK. Just look what Jill has done with it!' He lifted out a pink vest, expecting to see a smile on

154

Janet's lips, but for once she was not forthcoming when she saw the familiar carrier bag.

'Oh . . . laundry. I . . . I hadn't expected you to bring any more laundry, Hugh.' Her voice was reluctant, but she reached out for the bag. 'Well, perhaps, under the circumstances . . . just this once . . . ' She paused and silence fell.

Hugh was taken aback. Janet had always been so insistent in the past that she didn't mind at all doing his laundry. She had a good automatic machine and a tumble drier, and he had always seen to it that there was a discreet bonus in her pay check. Now he felt rather rebuffed by her manner.

'I'm sorry I asked, Janet,' he said rather stiffly, reaching out to retrieve the bag. 'I should have had more sense. I know you say it's not a great deal of work, but judging by Jill's long face yesterday morning, there's more work than a mere male realises. The underwear is really quite clean, even if it is pink. I'll just have to put up with it.'

Janet bit her lip.

'I don't think you quite understand. Hugh,' she said. 'It really is no trouble to me to do it, but . . . but I don't think I ought to do your laundry for you. It's difficult for me to explain, but I don't think I want you to become dependent on me again.'

'Dependent?' Hugh frowned. Was he really so dependent on Janet? He looked at her as she sat at her typewriter. She was so very competent, so self-assured, her hair shone and her skin had the warm richness of health and inner joy in living. Throughout his recent troubles, he had found her presence reassuring. Perhaps he did depend on her more than he ought.

'I hadn't realised I was becoming dependent on you, Janet,' he admitted, 'but you are quite right, I am. I . . . I feel rather ashamed that I've taken you so much for granted.'

'I don't mean that either, Hugh,' she said swiftly. 'Don't blame yourself.'

'But I should have seen — '

'No, it isn't you, Hugh. It's me . . . I don't want you to become too dependent on me. It just isn't a good idea, that's all.'

He turned away and began to put papers into his briefcase. He didn't want to part with Janet Fairbairn. She was not just an employee, she was a friend — she was more than a friend . . .

Hugh swallowed and thrust the thought firmly behind him. How could he even think such a thing? He was married to Anna, for better, for worse — for worse, as it had proved just recently.

But they were married and had a family . . .

'I — I'll see you later, Janet,' he said hurriedly.

'Leave the laundry, Hugh. I think Jill needs a little help to turn it white again.'

'No. There's no need,' Hugh began.

'Leave it,' I said.

'Well . . . If you're sure . . . '

'I'm sure.' She turned to look at him and their eyes held.

Hugh picked up his briefcase and hurried away.

* * *

The first postcard showing a view from the Acropolis at Athens arrived from Anna a few days later, and Jill propped it up on the mantelpiece. She stared at it longingly. If only she was with her mother and Aunt Helen in Greece . . .

The latest in Jill's series of domestic disasters had been to spill food in the bottom of the oven which had burnt and stuck fast. She had then proceeded to break one of her fingernails trying to scrub it clean and she was sitting on the floor trying to neaten the nail with scissors when the kitchen door opened and Adrian stuck his head round it.

'Anyone at home?' he asked. 'Do you always sit like that on the kitchen floor, Jill?'

'Only when I'm tired,' she explained, 'and I warn you, I'm not in a very good mood. I've just broken my nail on this stove.'

'Make some coffee then,' he coaxed. 'Look, I've brought along two chocolate eclairs. I thought I would find you ready for your elevenses.' He gave her a sympathetic smile.

'I've never been readier in my life,' she said, struggling to her feet. She laid the scissors down.

'I couldn't enjoy it in here, though, Adrian. Go into the sitting-room, and I'll bring the coffee.'

Adrian went through to the sitting-room and sat down on a chair by the fire. The daily paper was on a small table and he picked it up, then paused when he saw that it was open at the 'Situations Vacant' column.

Several situations had been ringed and Adrian noticed that a pad and pencil lay on the table, and that the pad had the words 'Draft Letter' written across the top.

Unashamedly, Adrian began to study

the situations. Jill had underlined the salaries which were being offered, and it was obvious that this was the primary consideration in each case. None of the jobs which attracted her had very worthwhile prospects.

Jill came through with the coffee and chocolate eclairs, then plumped herself down on the settee.

'Do you think one chocolate eclair will make me fat?' she asked.

'No, but I've no doubt you expect to grow fat on one of those jobs you've marked,' Adrian commented. 'It isn't the highest salary which necessarily makes the best career, Jill. And anyway, I thought you were going to think about medical training.'

'Don't start that again,' she said, 'and put my paper down. It's none of your business, Adrian. I'll be lucky to get any job these days. The competition is so fierce.'

'How do you know you would be turned down for medical school if you don't even try?'

'And how do you know what I want

to do with my life?' Jill demanded. 'One eclair doesn't give you the right to lecture me!'

'No, but being your friend does, surely. I can say what I think, can't I, Jill? You don't hesitate to tell me what you think at times.'

'Well, I'll tell you what I think now. I want a job where I can earn good money. I'm young and I want to live a little. I don't want to wait till I'm older. Suppose . . . suppose something happened, like what happened to Mum. My life would be over and I wouldn't ever have lived.

'How do you see the future, Adrian? Is it a lovely bright road with flowers on either side? Well, mine twists and turns and I'm afraid of what I can't see. I'm afraid of what will leap out at me round the next bend, or the next, or the next. I want something out of my life while I'm able to enjoy it.'

Adrian looked at her levelly.

'I wish I had taped that so that I could play it back to you, and let you listen to yourself. Really listen. None of us can see into the future, Jill. We just have to have a little faith, that's all. If you had to choose between having a good time and . . . and the love of a friend, which would you choose? Just think about that.'

She didn't answer. Her face wore the mulish look her mother would have recognised, and which Adrian had also seen once or twice.

'Thanks for the coffee, Jill,' he said quietly, and stood up, then the door clicked softly behind him.

★ ★ ★

'How did you manage to get your underwear white again, Daddy?' Jill asked at the breakfast table the following morning.

For once she, Peter and their father were all having breakfast at the same time.

Hugh flushed slightly and pretended to be deep in his paper.

'Daddy!'

'What . . . Oh, the laundry . . . Janet did it for me.'

Peter looked at him curiously. He knew his mother would not be at all pleased if she knew that Janet Fairbairn was doing his father's washing. They had all promised faithfully to do their own, but Jill had claimed she could manage it all.

'I'll use the washing machine tonight, Jill,' he offered. 'I don't mind taking a turn.'

Hugh moved uncomfortably. Was Peter beginning to make pointed remarks? He finished his coffee and rose to his feet.

'I'll be late tonight, Jill,' he told her.

'And I'll be early,' Peter said, as their father let himself out of the door. 'As a matter of fact, I'll have to do the washing later. I forgot, I'm going to Sharon Bell's flat again. I want to keep on at her until she talks to me.'

'Oh, for goodness' sake, let it go, Peter,' Jill said crossly.

'I can't. Why should I? I know she

was lying about Mum, and I'm not seeing our family broken up like this. Just look at Dad . . . '

Peter bit his lip and turned away. He had better not voice his suspicions to Jill, but his father was staying out late rather often. Was it really necessary to work so hard?

Peter gave himself a mental shake, and a flush of shame began to creep up his cheeks. What was happening to all of them? He was practically accusing his father of being unfaithful, just because his secretary had done his laundry. How neurotic could he get?

'What about Dad?' Jill was asking.

'Nothing really, just that he works too hard, that's all,' Peter ended lamely.

'I think he has the prospect of a big job,' Jill said. 'He's all excited about it.'

Peter nodded. Perhaps that was all. But because he had even suspected that something might be wrong proved to him that all was not well amongst them as a family. He should not be thinking such things about his father.

'I Don't Want
To Leave You'

Peter had given the matter a great deal of thought, and this time his approach to Sharon Bell was very different. In one hand he held a large bunch of flowers, and in the other a box of chocolates peeped from a white paper bag.

He had made no progress by hectoring Nurse Bell, but perhaps he could accomplish a great deal more if he chose a softer approach. For a moment as he stood looking at the girl who had opened the door, he didn't like himself very much, but he put all such thoughts firmly behind him and smiled pleasantly.

'Good evening, Nurse Bell.'

'Oh. Oh, it's you,' she said rather dully. 'I might have known you would come back.'

'Yes, I said I would, but this time I've brought a peace offering. Flowers and chocolates. And an apology. I had no right to try to bulldoze my way into your life, no right at all. I'm sorry.'

She stood back uncertainly, looking at the delightful pink roses and the box of chocolates.

'Please take them,' Peter invited.

'You'd better come in,' the girl said, stepping back.

Hurriedly, she picked up discarded clothing, magazines and coffee mugs after she had put down her flowers and chocolates on the coffee table.

'Er . . . would you like coffee?' she asked awkwardly.

'Yes, please.'

Peter sat down and, after a moment's hesitation, Sharon disappeared into the kitchen, and he could hear the swish of water and the rattle of cups on to a tray.

Peter looked round the sitting-room with interest. There was certainly no evidence of male occupation. An embroidery basket leaned against a chair by the fireside and a pile of fashion magazines spilled out of a rack near the television set.

'I'm afraid I only have crispbread biscuits,' Sharon apologised as she came back into the room.

'What could be nicer?' he asked.

For the first time she smiled a little, showing a pretty dimple in her cheek.

'Your chocolates,' she said ruefully. 'I've been trying to diet — I can put on weight so easily. Life is very unfair.'

'Yes, it is,' he agreed quietly, and saw the colour beginning to stain her cheeks. Her hands trembled as she poured the coffee and handed him a cup.

'I had thought that you would be married by now,' Peter said bluntly.

'No. My . . . my engagement was broken.'

Peter waited for her to say more, but there was only a heavy silence in the room.

'Your engagement was broken?' he prompted.

'I . . . my fiancé married someone else.'

'I'm sorry.' His voice was suddenly gentle and Sharon's eyes quickly filled with tears as she turned her head away and drank her coffee at a gulp.

'It's funny that we never met,' Peter said. 'When you and my mother were colleagues, I answered the phone occasionally when you rang to swap duties. I thought that perhaps it was because you wanted to keep a special date.'

'Perhaps. I . . . I don't remember.'

'But you do remember swapping duties?'

Her face was white.

'Why have you come, Mr Cameron?' she demanded.

'Please, call me Peter.' His mind was working swiftly. He was sure that he would get more out of Sharon if he was patient with her, yet it was a great temptation to stare her straight in the eyes and demand to know why she had lied at the trial. Because she had lied . . .

★   ★   ★

Now he smiled and turned towards the music centre.

'That looks interesting. Got any good records?' he said, changing the subject quickly.

'A few.'

'Don't you go out in the evenings? You mustn't be lonely just because you've broken your engagement. My girlfriend and I often go to the sports club, either for badminton or dancing. Why don't you come along some time?'

Her face had a closed look once more.

'Why ask me when you already have a partner?' she demanded, almost harshly. 'You know I would only be in the way.'

'Indeed you would not. You're my mother's friend and friends should always stick together.'

Again he saw the colour staining her cheeks, but with a cheerful smile he suddenly rose to his feet. Perhaps he had said enough for one evening.

'Thanks for the coffee, Sharon. That was nice,' he said pleasantly. 'Think over what I've said. You'd have a good time at our club. I'll call on you again in a day or two . . . '

'I don't want to go to any club!'

'Then we can play some records instead. I'm sure my mother wouldn't like to hear that you're lonely — she knows so well how it feels. Even the nicest people can let you down . . . people you would have trusted with your last penny, too!' he said firmly.

Sharon's face was as white as paper, her eyes staring.

'Stop it!' she whispered. 'Why can't you leave me alone? You . . . you're worse than Philip . . . '

'Who's Philip?'

'Philip McIver. He was always on at me. I wasn't to become involved. I was to keep out of everything. I was to say nothing . . . no phone calls, no change of duty, no anything. And I listened to him because I . . . I loved him, and believed that he knew best. And now look where I am!'

She turned round almost wildly.

'Now look at me! Later, when I saw I had been wrong . . . and he had been wrong, he wouldn't listen and he walked out on me. He went to someone else. Then you come, asking questions and telling me what to do. Why can't you all leave me alone?'

Peter's eyes had grown very bright, and rather hard.

'What did Philip McIver tell you to do, Sharon?' he asked quietly. 'Don't you think you had better tell me?'

'Nothing. There's nothing to tell. Please go. I . . . I haven't really been very well, you see, and I would just like an early night.'

Peter paused uncertainly. Already she had probably told him more than she realised, or had intended, and if he questioned her closely perhaps he could get to the root of the matter. He was sure she would admit to perjuring herself at the trial, and if so, what a homecoming gift to his mother that would be!

But another look at the girl stayed his tongue. She looked very white and tired and he believed her when she said she hadn't been feeling well.

★   ★   ★

Anna Cameron was thinking about her family as she wrote each of them a postcard, then she smiled as a shadow fell over the small table where she was working.

'I hope I'm not disturbing you.' Alan Haydon, the tall American with the greying hair whom she had met on the plane when they flew to Athens, slid easily into the chair beside her.

'Not at all, Alan. I'm just writing cards for Hugh and the children.' She smiled.

Aunt Helen was lying down after an excellent lunch, but Anna had gone up on deck, determined not to lose even one minute of this wonderful cruise.

'This card is for little Wendy, I see,' Alan said. 'She looks so like her grandmother. I cannot believe you are a grandmother, Anna.'

She blushed prettily and smiled at him. The sun had flecked her skin with gold, and her appetite had improved so that she was no longer the thin, rather anxious-looking woman who had waved goodbye to her family.

Alan Haydon had been very quick to notice that her heart was not always as light as it could be.

On the day they had visited Sounion, Aunt Helen had had to rest and had urged them to explore the place without her.

Together, Anna and Alan had wandered towards the beautiful Temple of Poseidon, and the sheer beauty and majesty of it all had made Anna catch her breath.

'It makes one's troubles seem small,' she had whispered.

'But no less important,' he said as he took her arm. 'Are your troubles so big,

Anna? You look very sad at times.'

Anna had hesitated. Castleden and Hugh seemed very far away, but their shadow continued to hang over her, even though she had been determined to put everything to the back of her mind, if only for Aunt Helen's sake.

She glanced at Alan Haydon. He was a professor of mathematics at a university in New York, and a year before he had lost his wife. In his own sadness and loneliness, he had recognised her troubled spirit, and soon she was pouring out all that had happened to her over the past year.

'You weren't to know the old lady was so weak,' he said quietly. 'My guess is that her time had come, even if you had sat by her bedside holding her hand. Your husband must be proud of you.'

The words had been unexpected and Anna could not hide the tell-tale expression on her face, showing him how wrong he was.

'It isn't easy for him,' she defended.

'Of course it isn't. It can't be easy for either of you. I guess your nice Aunt Helen is doing the right thing, bringing you on this trip. Why not take advantage of all this beauty and try to forget for a short while? Anna Cameron, as of this minute you and I have just come alive to enjoy ourselves. No past. Only present. You are a lovely lady and anyone would be proud to have your company. I'm sure glad it's me.'

The ship rode gently on the smooth clear gentle waves and Anna sighed. It was a long time since she had been so happy.

★   ★   ★

Jill's cheeks were flushed with excitement as she gathered the post together, having picked it up off the doormat. Swiftly she put one of the letters into the pocket of her jacket and hurried into the kitchen with the rest of the mail.

'Mum's sent us a card each,' she said happily. 'One for you, Daddy, with a letter, and a card each for Peter and me. Mmm . . . just look at these views! Doesn't it look like heaven?'

'It certainly does,' Peter agreed.

Jill gave him a second look. There was a barely-suppressed excitement about Peter which intrigued her. He had been up to something, she thought sagely, even though he was refusing to answer her probing questions. She had not pursued the matter, however, since she had her own secrets buried deep in her jacket pocket. She could hardly wait for the door to close behind her father and Peter before diving into her pocket to retrieve the letter.

It was typewritten and the envelope was an intriguing shade of jade green and of very good quality. It invited Miss Jill Cameron to attend an interview for the position of receptionist with Starlight Promotions at three o'clock on the ninth of the month. She should ask for Mr Dovey.

Jill's heart leapt. An interview at last! And that very afternoon! Her hands flew to her hair, and her mind became busy with what she ought to wear.

She was very nervous when she finally presented herself for her interview in the rather grand suite of offices near the centre of the town. No expense had been spared over the office fitments and when she was conducted into an inner office, a tall man with a smooth olive complexion and dark hair rose to greet her. She learned that she was the final applicant to be interviewed.

'Miss Jill Cameron,' he said. His voice was faintly accented, but Jill only noticed that his clothing was immaculate. He asked her many questions as to her age and qualifications. Before the interview ended Jill took a deep breath.

'I think I had better tell you, Mr Dovey,' she said shakily, 'my mother has recently been discharged from an open prison. The circumstances were these . . . '

His black eyes never left her face as

she described what had happened, and when she had finished speaking, he leaned back in his chair and regarded her thoughtfully.

'I do not regard that as a problem, Miss Cameron,' he said at length. 'We are a big organisation setting up a franchise scheme in this area. I think you would make an excellent receptionist when we interview potential clients.'

Jill's heart hammered with relief. She had been honest and it did not appear to matter.

'I will write to you confirming the appointment and salary,' he promised, and Jill left the office walking on air. She would show Adrian that she was quite capable of finding herself a splendid job.

★ ★ ★

At that moment, Elizabeth Caldwell would have noticed a great likeness between Peter and his sister. He, too, wore an expression of suppressed excitement as he described his visit to Sharon Bell.

'I've invited her to come dancing with us,' he said eagerly, 'and not just because I want to soften her up. I think she needs to be taken out of herself, Elizabeth. She's far too withdrawn. Maybe, when she goes out among people again, she'll realise that she's living an unnatural life and she'll want to make a fresh start. That's the best chance we'll have of getting her to tell us the truth.'

He turned to her and she smiled a little without comment.

Peter hardly noticed that Elizabeth's enthusiasm was not quite as great as his own.

'I thought we could ask her for Saturday. What do you say?' he asked.

'Ask her for Saturday by all means, Peter,' she said quietly, 'but you can count me out. There are quite a few things which can keep me busy on Saturday and I think it would really be much better if you and Sharon just went to the club on your own.'

Some of the eagerness left Peter's eyes.

'Don't be like that, Elizabeth,' he protested. 'You know why I'm doing this. I'm sure Sharon will come much more readily if she has the company of both of us. That's what I promised her.'

'Well you had no right to make promises on my behalf,' she said evenly. 'Anyway, I want to go home to Edinburgh this weekend. I . . . I had rather thought you might like to come with me, but I appreciate that seeing Sharon is more important . . . '

'I have to do it, Elizabeth,' he said, and his eyes pleaded for her understanding.

'Yes, I know you do,' she said quietly, 'but you'll have to do it without my help, Peter. I'm sorry.'

Peter nodded as he turned to go. This time he did not kiss Elizabeth good night and her eyes were sad as she watched him go.

The rain started just before Peter got

home and he ran the short distance from the bus, racing into the kitchen as Jill was boiling up some milk for a hot drink.

'Just in time.' Peter grinned. 'What a night! Isn't Dad home yet?'

'Not yet,' Jill said. 'I shan't wait up, though. He has his own key.'

'I'll have to spread out my coat over the chair,' Peter said, 'then I'm off to bed, too.'

★　★　★

Hugh was deathly tired. He and Janet Fairbairn had put in one of the heaviest days of their lives. All afternoon they had worked together on the supermarket reconstruction plans, then Janet had suggested that they go back to her flat for a quick meal.

'We can finish the job if we really stick at it, Hugh,' she suggested. 'It should be in by tomorrow, don't forget.'

'I know,' he agreed, 'but I honestly didn't realise there was so much still to be ironed out, and so much typing in the completed estimate.'

'Don't worry about that,' she said, almost impatiently. 'I can soon do the actual typing. But I need you to give me the figures. We've got to work together on it, Hugh, or a great deal of time is wasted.'

'You're quite right. OK, Janet, if you don't mind . . . ?'

'I don't mind,' she said, smiling. 'I'll be as glad to see the job finished as you. You know, Hugh, I've got a strange feeling about this. Somehow I just know you're going to land this contract. I've felt it right from the beginning.'

'I hope you're right, Janet,' he said. 'I know what you mean, though. Everything has fitted so well into place that I feel we can't go wrong. The only thing is . . . it'll be very disappointing if the work is all for nothing.'

'Now don't start being downhearted. That's only because you're tired. I'll make us a quick meal. Bacon and eggs will do and we can eat in the kitchen.'

Janet's kitchen was as neat as her work. It was a matter of minutes to set the table and make the tea.

'I'll wash up while you type those pages up to date,' Hugh offered after their meal.

He gathered together his final notes and Janet remained sitting at her typewriter. But even then it was almost two hours before she typed the last sheet, and the beautifully neat, important folder was put into Hugh's executive case for delivery in the morning.

'I'll get us a hot drink before you go,' Janet said after she had put away her typewriter. 'I feel exhilarated, but — '

'Tired to death at the same time!' Hugh put in.

He spread out his long legs in front of the fire, then as Janet brought the hot drinks in hand-thrown mugs, the heavy rain began to lash the windows and she turned a concerned face to him, having peeped round the curtains.

'Goodness, Hugh, what a night! And

we walked round from the office. Your car is still there.'

'Maybe it will pour itself out fairly quickly,' he said. 'I feel as though I can't worry about a thing tonight.'

She pulled up a small table for their mugs and sat down beside him.

'I have a pain in my left shoulder with typing,' she said, trying to reach round to the back of her neck to ease the muscles.

His arm went round her shoulders and his long fingers massaged the place.

'Is that better?'

'Mmm. Just half an inch down.'

'For you, anything. You know, I'd never have done it without you, my dear. If everything goes according to plan . . . ' His voice tailed away as she turned to smile at him, then his arm tightened about her shoulders.

His gratitude towards her went very deep and he leaned forward to kiss her cheek. Then suddenly they were looking deeply into one another's eyes and it was Janet's soft quivering mouth which

Hugh found under his own.

Everything else was forgotten as he began to kiss her. She resisted for a moment, then with a sigh, she relaxed in his arms, and it seemed as though they were the only two people in the world.

Hugh had felt Janet's tiny movement of protest, but it was so long since he had held anyone in his arms like this that he pulled her closely against him. Then once again he was kissing her passionately, feeling the softness of her hair against his skin. There was a warm, sweet smell of her in his nostrils and her skin felt cool and fresh.

'Janet!' he whispered hoarsely. 'Oh, Janet . . . I . . . I don't want to go. I don't want to leave you.'

He clung to her desperately and when she replied her voice was so muffled that he could scarcely hear it.

'Hugh, you needn't . . . you . . . can stay . . . '

Was Peter Responsible?

Jill had called her father twice and Peter three times before she realised that Hugh hadn't come home. She peeped into his bedroom, then shook Peter once again.

'Get up, Peter. You're going to be late!'

'I'll wait till Dad's had the bathroom.'

'He hasn't come home. He must have forgotten to tell me, but I'll ring the office just to make sure he's OK. Did he say he was going to Edinburgh, Peter?'

Peter glanced at the time, then forgot everything else in the need to get to his work on time.

'There's no reply from the office,' she said to Peter when he arrived in the kitchen.

'Try again, later,' he advised.

Jill had made him a bacon sandwich,

which he munched between looking for his ballpoint pen and asking Jill for change for bus fares.

'I'll open the door for you,' she offered.

The postman was coming up the path and Jill grabbed the mail and leafed through it swiftly. There was a letter for her in the familiar green envelope and her heart leapt with anticipation.

'Nothing for you, Peter,' she called after her brother. 'Nobody loves you.'

He made a face and she retreated into the house and stacked up her father's mail on the sideboard.

Then she opened her own letter and exclaimed with excitement and delight when she saw it confirmed her appointment with Starlight Enterprises — and the salary she could expect.

If only the whole family had been at home. She longed to share such wonderful news with someone, and tried Myra's number. As sisters they weren't always very close, but Jill suspected that even Myra would be impressed when she mentioned the salary.

There was no reply and Jill was hanging up the receiver when her father dashed into the house.

'Oh, Daddy!' she cried with delight. 'I am glad to see you. I've got something to show you.'

She held out the letter, but Hugh waved it away.

'Sorry, dear, it'll have to wait till later. I've been held up and I've got a very important appointment to keep. I want to freshen up.' He was already halfway up the stairs.

Jill sat down, slightly deflated. In record time her father reappeared, picked up his post and nodded to her swiftly.

'See you tonight some time. Cheerio, Jill.'

The house closed in silently around Jill as the sounds of Hugh's footsteps receded, and she sighed.

She picked up the telephone and

dialled Adrian's number.

'Is there any chance you might be around my way later on?' she asked. 'Would you care to drop in for some coffee, Adrian? I've got something I want to show you.'

'I'll be delighted to call in,' Adrian said. 'See you.'

'See you,' Jill echoed.

Later, Adrian knocked lightly on the kitchen door, then pushed it open.

'Come in,' Jill said happily. 'You're just in time. I've got coffee and biscuits all ready. We'll go into the sitting-room, then you can read my letter.'

'What letter?' Adrian asked.

'This one,' she said with triumph, producing the green envelope. 'You go on in there, and read that. I'll be with you in a sec.'

Adrian slid the letter out of the envelope and a small exclamation escaped his lips as he looked at the costly headed paper, and began to read the letter.

'Impressive, isn't it?' Jill asked, her

eyes shining as she put down the tray of coffee.

Adrian's heart sank.

'I know about these people, Jill,' he said quietly. 'Starlight Enterprises aren't new to me.'

'So?' She looked at him enquiringly.

'Nothing to their good.' He looked concerned.

Jill drew back, her eyebrows almost meeting in a frown.

'I might have known . . . ' she began.

'Just listen to me for a moment,' Adrian said swiftly. 'I know what I'm talking about. The directors of Starlight Enterprises have come very close to being jailed. They've already worked just such an enterprise as the one they're setting up here — in London. You know Gerry Morrison, my best friend? He's a doctor in London.

'Well, I stayed with him for a few days a couple of months ago and he arrived home in the early hours one morning, just about out on his feet. He'd been hours in the hospital, fighting for a man's life — unsuccessfully. He learned later that the man had put his life's savings into a Starlight Enterprise franchise scheme ... and lost every penny. He was sure he was founding the family fortunes, but when it didn't materialise, the poor chap couldn't face his wife.

* * *

Dully Jill listened to what he had to say. It couldn't be true, she thought. A short time ago she had been in an ecstasy of delight at her good fortune, and now Adrian was tearing it to shreds and throwing it at her feet.

'I'm so sorry to hurt you like this,' he said huskily, drawing her into his arms. 'Of course you're worth that salary and more, but you'll have to dig your plot of ground for it first. Don't you see that?'

'Why did I show it to you?' Jill asked tearfully.

'When you've considered it a little more, you'll thank your lucky stars that you did. Look, Jill, I didn't like having to tell you about that firm. I would love to have been able to be happy with you because I love you.'

She moved away from him.

'Oh, don't go leaping away. I know we're maybe too young to be really in love, but that might come one day, Jill, and that's why I want to stay in your life. I . . . I hope you understand what I'm trying to say.'

The tears were beginning to dry on Jill's cheeks as she stared at Adrian. He had come into her life almost like another brother — and she couldn't quite grasp what he was saying. A tear rolled down her cheek, and Adrian wiped it with his handkerchief.

'Just think about it all, Jill,' he said gently. 'Don't make a mistake. You've already seen how easy it is to do that. I've got to go now, but I'll be back for you tonight. We'll go out somewhere, even if it is only for a walk. OK?'

'OK,' she echoed, and he bent and kissed her swiftly.

Jill sat still and quiet after he had gone, her letter clutched in her lap. It would certainly have to be carefully considered. If only her mother was home . . .

$\star \quad \star \quad \star$

Anna's thoughts had never been further from her family . . . Accompanied by Alan Haydon, she and Aunt Helen had gone ashore at Rhodes and although the island was crowded with holiday-makers, they had managed to visit the Grand Master's Castle which was once the home of the Knights of St John.

'Bodrun in the morning,' Aunt Helen said the following evening. 'We must be up early for that. I want to buy a pair of camel shoes for myself. If you don't mind, I'll retire early. We'll soon be back to Athens now.'

The words had brought a slight chill to Anna's heart. Soon the cruise would be over and she did not want it to end. She wanted it to last . . . and last . . .

Alan Haydon's hand squeezed hers as they sat at a small table on deck. There had been dancing after dinner and she and Alan had danced until they were tired. Now it astonished her that he could so swiftly sense her mood.

'Let's walk over to the rail and look at the moonlight on the sea,' he said softly. 'It's a sight not to be missed, and this is the sort of evening which we'll always want to remember.'

Anna forgot everything else as she took his hand and together they strolled over to a quiet part of the rail, and Anna looked out on to a sea of enchantment such as she had never thought possible.

'I've often wondered what heaven would be like,' she whispered. 'Now I know.'

Alan's arm slipped round her shoulders, then suddenly she was leaning up against him and he was holding her as though it were the most natural thing in the world.

'I've never loved another woman,

except my wife . . . until now,' he told her in a low voice. 'You are very beautiful to me, Anna.'

He bent and kissed her.

'Maybe I had no right to do that, but I'm not going to apologise. I don't know what's going to happen in the future, Anna, but nothing can take these few days away from me. It's not just the trip, my dear, I've been on many such trips and made many new friends, but I knew straightaway that you are going to mean something special to me.'

'Oh, Alan!' Anna's eyes misted with tears.

'Just think about the present,' he said urgently. 'We mustn't miss a minute of all this beauty we're sharing together.'

Faintly they could hear the sounds of music and the happy sounds of laughter and cheerful conversation.

'I don't want it to end,' Anna confessed, 'but having said that, I know I'm speaking like a spoilt child. It must all end, and soon.'

'I hope you're talking about the cruise,' Alan said. 'Your hair looks so lovely in the moonlight. And your eyes. But your skin is pearly-white and so perfect that I'm afraid you are not real!'

She laughed, her eyes bright with the pleasure of hearing such words of admiration. It seemed to be a very long time since anyone had thought her beautiful enough to tell her so and she thought wistfully of her husband.

She shivered, and Alan held her close.

'There's a chill breeze in spite of all the beauty. I can't have you catching cold. Shall we walk back to the cabins?'

'I think we'd better,' Anna said, laughing a little.

They strolled back, laughing and talking, but even as they neared Alan's cabin, Anna knew she was being asked a question and must find an answer.

Once again a quick look into his eyes was enough for understanding each other's heart, and the new feeling in her wanted to urge her to forget everything else but this wonderful night, and this man who had come to mean so much to her.

Then, suddenly, Anna was pushing him away.

'No, Alan, it's no use . . . I can't,' she whispered. 'I just can't. It . . . it isn't me, somehow. I don't know how to explain, but — '

'But you needn't explain one word,' he said gently. 'Not one word. You see, the reason why you can't come to me is the very reason why you mean so much to me. It's because you are true and fine, my Anna. Maybe you never will be mine, but no-one can take away my feelings for you.'

He took her arm and together they walked towards the cabin Anna shared with Aunt Helen. Outside, Alan kissed her again.

'That's for good night,' he said. 'I'll see you in the morning.'

'Good night,' Anna echoed softly.

★ ★ ★

Peter had been upset at Elizabeth's attitude whenever he mentioned Sharon Bell's name. She claimed to understand what he was trying to do, but she didn't like it, nor did she approve.

'Tell me what you would do,' he had invited. 'I know now I'm getting somewhere with Sharon. She's beginning to make mistakes. Already she's put her foot in it and has admitted to having telephone conversations with Mum, and swapping duties. At the trial, she said that never happened. That's one lie for a start.'

'Oh, Peter! Don't you see? It . . . it's sort of underhand, somehow, all this sort of thing. I don't like to see you making friends with her just to . . . to hound her.'

'I'm not hounding her,' Peter objected. 'In fact, I think I'm doing a good job for Sharon, calling to see her like this. She needs to be taken out of herself.'

'Then you'll do a much better job without me,' Elizabeth said, 'but I still feel as though you . . . you're spying on her.'

'That's an ugly word,' Peter protested.

'Oh, I'm sorry,' Elizabeth said. 'Believe me, Peter, I am sorry and I do understand why you're doing it, but . . . but it just doesn't feel right.'

'You and our Jill!' Peter said explosively. 'You don't help at all, either of you. All you have are feelings. Well, my parents had feelings, too, for each other and now I'm afraid for them. I'm afraid in case they lose those feelings and never get them back.'

He was still thinking over those words as he sat in the bus which would take him to Sharon's flat. Was he being stupid and imaginative when he thought that his father had a motive other than business for staying away from home?

Peter felt uncomfortable. He hated himself for harbouring such thoughts but they persisted nevertheless. How much did his parents still love one another? How much did the family mean to them now?

Peter leapt off the bus and began to walk towards Sharon's flat with a white, set face. He and Sharon Bell needed one another. She needed to be shaken out of the life she was leading, and he needed to hear from her that his mother was neither selfish nor uncaring. She had done her job that day as competently and thoughtfully as she always had done it, and his father should see that their troubles were not her fault.

There was no answer to his ring at the bell, but Sharon was in all right, he could see a faint glow of light through the glass door.

Peter rang the bell twice more, each time keeping his finger on the button, then listening carefully.

He lifted the letter-box and shouted through it — 'Sharon! I know you're in there! Open the door! It's Peter!'

There was a dull, faint sound inside the flat, and an indistinct moaning sound which was almost like a whisper.

Peter stood uncertainly for a moment then, taking off his shoe, he smashed a small pane of glass above the handle of the door.

Protecting his hand with a handkerchief, he managed to reach in and turn the key. The door flew open and Peter ran into the living-room.

With every nerve tingling, he stopped in the doorway. Sharon lay face downwards on the floor in front of the settee.

For a moment, Peter paused in the doorway, then he rushed forward and knelt down beside her, gently turning her over. She was deeply unconscious, her breathing unnatural, and Peter's heart beat rapidly when he saw that a bottle which had contained tablets lay empty on the settee.

Fear lent power to his limbs as he reached for the telephone and dialled 999. Briskly and efficiently, though his voice trembled with shock, he managed to give all the necessary details, then turned his attention to Sharon once more, uncertain how to render first aid.

It seemed hours instead of minutes before the ambulance men arrived and made a brief but efficient examination, then Sharon was quickly bundled on to a stretcher and one of the ambulance men asked Peter if he was a relative.

'Only a friend. I . . . I don't think she has many relatives,' he said.

'Better come with us, sir,' the man said, briskly.

★   ★   ★

Peter was shown into a waiting-room after he had given the nurse all the details about Sharon he could remember, including the fact that she had been his mother's colleague in private nursing. This would help to trace her personal details and any medical records which were required.

'And you can think of no reason why she should want to take an overdose of sleeping tablets?' the staff nurse asked with a direct look. Peter had taken along the bottle which he had found on the settee.

'I . . . I didn't know her well enough,' he said at length. 'Her engagement was broken recently. I suppose she was unhappy.'

Sharon had been wheeled away, and all he wanted to know was what was happening and whether she was conscious.

'Will I know soon . . . how she is, I mean?' he asked the nurse.

'We'll let you know as soon as there's news,' she told him gently. 'Why don't you go and have a cup of tea, Mr Cameron?'

But Peter's limbs were beginning to feel heavy, and as he glanced at the time, he suddenly realised it was quite late. He would have to telephone Jill.

It was Adrian who answered the telephone.

'Jill's making toast for supper,' he explained. 'What's the problem, Peter?'

'I'm at the hospital,' Peter said hoarsely, then cleared his throat.

'What's happened?' Adrian asked urgently.

'It's Sharon . . . Sharon Bell. She . . . she's taken an overdose of sleeping pills.' Again his voice grew hoarse as he explained the circumstances, and Adrian's voice came clearly and crisply.

'Stay there. I'm coming to fetch you, I've got the car.'

He put down the receiver as Jill walked into the sitting-room, carrying a plate of savoury toast and two mugs of coffee on a tray.

'Who was on the phone?' she asked.

'Peter,' Adrian said quietly. 'He's at the hospital . . . '

'Hospital!' Jill cried.

'Now, don't panic. Everything's under control. Apparently he found Sharon Bell unconscious at her flat. He called an ambulance.'

'Oh, how awful!' Jill exclaimed. 'What was wrong with her?'

'Overdose of sleeping pills.'

Jill's face went pale. 'I told Peter not to start questioning her. Now look what's happened!'

'That's enough, Jill.' Adrian gripped her arm. 'Peter's in a bad enough state over it without you throwing wild accusations around. I'm going round to the hospital to bring him back home, even if we have to wait an hour or two.'

'I'm coming with you,' Jill said.

Adrian nodded agreement.

'OK, get your coat. It can be quite chilly at night.'

A Happy Memory

When Hugh arrived only a few minutes after Jill's departure with Adrian, he found the house even more empty and quiet than usual since it bore evidence of hasty departure. A plate of savoury toast and two mugs of coffee, still warm, were sitting on a small table in the lounge. Where were Jill and Peter, he wondered. Why had they left the house so suddenly?

How had he got his life into such a mess, Hugh wondered. That afternoon he and Janet had managed to clear quite a backlog of work which had been put to one side while they were working on the estimate for the big supermarket job. Now the estimate and plans had been presented and Hugh could only wait for a decision.

'We must get the VAT accounts up to date,' Janet insisted, 'and there are a few bills to be sent out.'

'I know.' Hugh hesitated, then he put aside his paperwork. 'Janet, we must talk, you and I, about . . . about us . . . '

Janet sighed, then laid aside her ballpoint pen. She had known that, sooner or later, she and Hugh would have to talk it out, and she realised she had come to a crossroads in her life.

Over the lunch hour she had sat quietly in the office and faced the fact that she had fallen very deeply in love with Hugh. She had also realised that she would never be the same to him as Anna.

She liked and admired Anna Cameron and had never blamed her in any way for trying to do her best for her family on the day Mrs Foster died. She was a responsible woman and Janet had always felt that Anna must have tried to do her best for everyone in the circumstances.

Anna and Hugh had been married for twenty-five years and nothing could take that away. Janet was firm in her resolution that she must do nothing more to hurt Anna Cameron.

Now Hugh was looking at her anxiously, and Janet turned to him forcing herself to meet his eyes.

'I think we must both forget about last night, Hugh,' she said, quietly. 'It . . . it was just something that happened, but it's in the past now. It must never happen again.'

The look of relief on his face was more painful to her than she could have believed, but it served to harden Janet's resolution evenmore. She had not read his feelings wrongly.

'I . . . I feel I have let you down,' he said, in a low voice.

She closed her eyes for a moment, then gently put her hand on his arm. 'Don't even think that, Hugh. When I say that we should forget it ever happened, I don't think we ever shall, but I think we ought to get it into perspective. I . . . I shan't ever forget but it . . . it was only an incident in our lives. Let's just make it a happy memory, but nothing more.'

He gazed at her searchingly, then his eyes cleared and it was the Hugh she had always known before who smiled at her this time.

'Thanks, Janet. It's so ... so inadequate but . . . thanks.'

Shortly afterwards, he left for home, and Janet, too, walked back to her flat. The light shower of rain mingled with her tears.

The house felt very empty to Hugh and he began to think about Anna, and to wonder when she would telephone to let him know she was back in London.

According to her postcards, the holiday would soon be finished and as Hugh leaned back in his chair, he could almost hear her light, cheerful voice talking to him from the kitchen as she prepared their evening meal. How long ago was it since they had really talked together? How far they had drifted apart!

It seemed a long time since he had been able to sit down and think about his life. He had no idea where his children might have gone this evening. He hardly knew what their interests were these days. His thoughts became so painful that he jumped to his feet and switched on the television, trying to concentrate on the programme.

★   ★   ★

Then he heard Adrian's car pulling up at the door, and with some relief he hurried to open it.

Jill was coming up the path with her arm through Peter's, having turned to assure Adrian that all was well and they would manage fine by themselves.

'Where have you been?' Hugh demanded, with a touch of irritation. 'I've been sitting here worrying myself — '

'I'm sorry, Daddy,' Jill broke in, contritely, 'but Peter needs to go up to bed.'

'What's wrong?' Hugh asked, as he saw his son's white face.

'I'm OK now,' Peter said, 'but if you don't mind, I . . . I'd just like to go up to bed. I had a little bit of bad news, that's all.'

'What sort of bad news?'

Jill took her father's arm and led him back into the sitting-room while Peter mounted the stairs to his bedroom. He felt deathly tired. It seemed a lifetime since he had rushed out of the house that morning in his usual hurry to get to work. How strange that he had not the slightest premonition as to how the day would end!

Peter tore off his clothes, and crawled into bed, but his mind was too confused for sleep. He kept re-living the awful moment when he had first seen Sharon Bell lying on the floor. Even as he had picked up the empty pill bottle, he had experienced a fierce pang of guilt which he had quickly suppressed.

But now it could no longer be ignored. He could not lie to himself. He was responsible for the girl's action. It was he who had driven her to take this step. He had kept at her, always turning the conversation and fastening on to the smallest detail about the day Mrs Foster died, in order to get her to admit the truth.

She must have been lonely and afraid, trying to cope with a broken engagement and the need to rebuild her life, and his intrusion must have been the last straw.

★   ★   ★

Once again Peter heard himself answering questions at the hospital and pleading ignorance of Sharon's motives. He had felt sick with nerves as he waited for news, then the staff nurse had come to find him and to tell him that Sharon was showing signs of recovery.

'She will be a very sick girl for a day or two,' the nurse said, 'but she still has her life, thanks to you, Mr Cameron. It was fortunate indeed that you decided to call and see her this evening. If she had lain there much longer . . . '

Peter had mumbled a reply, then Adrian and Jill were there to help him to the car. Adrian drove him to his own home, where he gave him hot sweet tea and the sort of bracing support which he needed. Thanks to Adrian, he had looked on it all more rationally, but he couldn't hide from himself that he was responsible for Sharon's attempted suicide.

'You were right,' he said to Jill. 'You and Elizabeth Caldwell, but you've got to believe me when I tell you that I never imagined in a million years anything like this would happen. That I would hound her until — '

Peter had felt so weak and tired that he had wanted to weep.

'How will Sharon feel when . . . when she does come round?' he asked. 'It will be an awful shock to her when she had expected to end it all.'

'There are trained staff to take care of that, Peter,' Adrian said. 'It's not your worry. Bed for you now.'

Old Dr Scott had given him a sedative and Peter's eyelids began to droop in sleep, but his last thoughts were of Sharon, lying so ill in hospital, then Elizabeth Caldwell. What would Elizabeth say when she learned what had happened? He should have listened to her. And, most of all, what would his mother say? She would have to know his motives for seeking out Sharon, and she would not like that at all.

*   *   *

Downstairs Jill had gone back into the sitting-room with her father.

'I'm sorry I didn't leave you a note, Daddy,' she apologised, 'but I forgot. I'm never very sure what time you'll be home these days.'

Hugh frowned. Was Jill's tone a trifle accusing?

'You know I've been busy,' he said sharply.

'Of course.' She nodded. Swiftly, she explained the circumstances, and Hugh

214

looked at her in bewilderment.

'Sharon Bell?' he asked. 'Wasn't she the young nurse who used to work with your mother?'

'Right,' Jill said. 'Peter got the idea she hadn't been telling the truth at the trial, and he decided to find her. He was worried, you see, about you and — ' she hesitated.

'What was Peter worried about?' he asked quickly. 'What about me? I fail to see the connection between Sharon Bell and myself, Jill.'

'It was nothing, really,' she said lamely.

'You must have had something in mind,' her father pursued.

Jill swallowed. Her father was staring at her, determined to be given an answer.

'Only that you and Mum seemed to have become — well — rather at odds with one another. Not quite as close as you used to be. I advised Peter to leave well alone and not to interfere,' she went on with a rush. 'I know you and

Mum are OK really. Deep down, I mean. Peter and I shouldn't worry. But we did, a little. Peter sees bogies everywhere — like that night you didn't come home . . . '

Her voice tailed off and her eyes were dark with distress when she saw how white her father looked.

'Daddy?' she whispered.

'It's all right, Jill,' he said in a low voice. 'Go to bed, dear. I'll see Peter in the morning.'

Slowly Jill turned away. He had not answered her question about her mother, and Jill's knees shook as she went up to bed. Was Peter right, then, that her parents were drifting apart? How upset her father had looked!

Slow, painful tears filled Jill's eyes and she longed for her mother to come home.

Hugh was up first the following morning, having spent a very poor night. He was anxious about Peter as he realised, even more than Jill, what a shock his son must have received when he found Sharon Bell in such a state.

When he woke in the morning, he slipped downstairs and made himself a cup of hot tea, then rang the hospital to inquire after Sharon. He learned that she was 'comfortable' and sighed a little with relief.

Pouring another cup of hot tea, he mounted the stairs to Peter's room, knocking gently on the door before pushing it open.

Peter woke immediately, his eyes unfocused, then he sat up when he saw his father.

'Dad! Is everything OK?' he put a hand to his forehead. 'Oh, goodness, I remember now, Sharon — '

'No need to worry, Peter,' Hugh interrupted, putting down the tray with the cup of tea. 'Jill told me all about it and I've telephoned the hospital for you. She's 'comfortable'. That means she's holding her own at any rate. Here, drink this tea. I'll ring your firm for you if you feel you can't make it today.'

'No, I must go to work. There are

things I really have to see to.'

Hugh nodded, glad to see that Peter looked brighter than he had anticipated.

'If you're sure you're well enough,' he began awkwardly. 'I . . . I'll get you some breakfast, Peter.'

'Sure. I'll be fine,' Peter said. 'I'll have a shower and that will blow off the cobwebs. Thanks, Dad.'

Peter felt better after his shower. Having dressed himself in clean clothing, he ran downstairs to the kitchen.

It was strange to see his father there, still clad in his dressing-gown, but Peter was glad of his support.

'I've put an egg on to boil for your breakfast,' Hugh said.

'I don't really feel very hungry,' Peter said, rubbing his forehead. His head still felt woolly.

'You'd better eat it now that I've made it for you. There goes Jill into the bathroom! She can sort things out in here. I'm never very sure of myself in the kitchen.'

Peter was conscious of an awkwardness between his father and himself. There were so many questions to be asked. His father must know why he had sought out Sharon, yet he hadn't even demanded an explanation. Instead they avoided one another's eyes.

★　★　★

It was a relief to hear Jill rushing downstairs, clad in her old jeans and jersey with her hair still a little untidy. She paused in the hallway as the post rattled through the letterbox.

'More postcards and letters from Mum and Aunt Helen,' she said, as she carried the mail into the kitchen. 'Bills for you, Dad, and a letter addressed to Mum. Aunt Helen seems enamoured of that man, Alan Haydon, yet Mum hardly mentions him. I wonder if Aunt Helen has found an elderly beau . . . What's wrong, Peter?'

Peter had gasped audibly as his eyes fell on the letter for his mother, and he picked it up, staring at it fixedly.

'What is it, Peter?' his father repeated.

Peter's heart was thudding. He had seen that distinctive backhand writing before.

'It — it's from Sharon Bell,' he said, almost in a whisper.

Jill's eyes were wide as she stared at Peter, then turned to look at her father, who was holding out his hand for the letter.

'Are you sure, Peter?' she asked.

Peter nodded. 'It's Sharon's writing all right. She's left-handed so she always writes with that backhand slope.'

His lips felt dry and he ran his tongue over them. Why had she written to his mother? Perhaps . . . perhaps she had decided to tell the truth about the evidence she gave at the trial.

At one time, Peter would have been overjoyed at the thought, but now all he could see was the girl's soft, curly hair clustered about her forehead as she lay on the floor in her flat.

'Shouldn't we open it?' he asked his

father. 'Perhaps the doctors at the hospital should know her state of mind just — just before she took those sleeping pills.'

Hugh turned the letter over in his hands.

'It's addressed to your mother,' he said to Peter. 'It would be different if Sharon had died. Then I expect the police would have wanted to see this immediately.'

Peter's face paled at the thought.

'Thank God she didn't,' he said fervently.

'I know.' Hugh nodded soberly. 'Your mother expects to be home in another couple of days. I think we ought to leave it for her with the rest of the mail.'

'I agree,' Jill said. 'I think she'd hate it if we opened any of her letters. Oh, Daddy, I'll be so glad to see Mum home again.'

'So will I,' Peter echoed.

Peter decided to have a quick cup of coffee before heading off for work. The day seemed to stretch ahead endlessly.

He would call at the hospital that evening, but if Sharon couldn't see him, then he would go and see Elizabeth. What would she say when she heard his news? She had warned him often enough to leave well alone.

Putting down his empty mug, Peter picked up his briefcase and made for the nearest bus stop. It was always quiet in the house, thought Jill, after the men had gone. Thank goodness it was only two more days before her mother came home.

Jill knew that she would have to think very deeply about her future after her mother returned. It didn't lie in studying medicine, thought Jill honestly. She was deeply interested in medicine but she was not the stuff good doctors were made of.

Adrian, not she, was just that sort of person.

Her cheeks grew pink as she began to get through the daily chores. He had told her he wanted her to think about marriage between them some time in the future, and Jill hugged that thought in her most secret heart. Did Adrian really care about her that much? If, after he qualified, he still felt the same, she would be so happy to be his wife . . .

★ ★ ★

Jill was startled out of her thoughts by the ringing of the telephone. She switched off the vacuum cleaner and rushed to answer it. Perhaps it was Adrian . . .

'Hello,' she said rather breathlessly.

'Hello, darling,' her mother said. 'I'm back in London with Aunt Helen . . . Hello . . . Jill?'

'Oh, Mum . . . ' Jill whispered, and there was so much tearful relief in her voice that Anna was startled.

'What's wrong, dear?' she asked. 'You sound upset.'

'Oh no, Mum, everything is fine now,' Jill said.

'I suppose your father isn't there?'

'No, he's gone to work, but I've got strict instructions to copy down the time of your train and Daddy will be there to meet you at Carlisle. Oh, Mum, I'm so glad you're home.'

After Anna had told Jill the train's arrival time at Carlisle and answered a few of her excited questions, she put down the telephone thoughtfully. There had been more in Jill's voice than merely pleasure at her mother's return.

She sighed as she went into the lounge to find Aunt Helen. It had been a marvellous holiday, but she was not altogether sorry that it had ended. In her handbag she had a note of Alan Haydon's address and she had promised faithfully to contact him if she ever needed a friend.

There was still a great deal of happiness for her to gain from life, and if her family was reluctant to share that happiness with her, then she must gather them towards her once more with the warmth of her own love.

Nor should she shut out Hugh

because of her own pride. It might take time for them to grow close once more, but Anna felt that it was worthwhile making the effort on her part, and being very patient if she did not have immediate success.

'Now, now, Anna,' Aunt Helen said, leaning forward as she began to pour the tea she had ordered in the hotel lounge. 'You look worried already, dear. You've been so much your old self recently. Don't worry, I'm sure Hugh and the children will be delighted to have you back.'

Anna smiled.

'You're a fairy godmother, Aunt Helen. You knew all along this holiday would breathe new life into me, didn't you?'

'I hope it has, dear.'

'It has,' Anna promised, and it seemed to her that she and Aunt Helen understood one another perfectly.

Full Of Excuses

Jill's relief at hearing her mother's voice had been great, and she was pleasantly surprised to see that her labours of the morning were beginning to pay off. The house looked much brighter and tidier than she would have believed. It was just as Adrian said. She was gaining experience and soon she might even start to enjoy being a housewife.

Jill longed to speak to him, but he wouldn't be at home today. He was taking the last of his examinations and though he was nervous and anxious, it was she who had been a prop to him for a change.

'You'll sail through, Adrian,' she said. 'It's in your blood. Just look at your grandfather.'

'I know,' he said dolefully. 'That's just it! I have so much to live up to.'

For the first time she had kissed him

226

of her own volition, then blushed a little. But Adrian had returned the kiss in full measure.

'Thanks, Jill darling,' he said. 'You don't know what that did for me.'

Jill phoned Hugh's office and left a message with Janet Fairbairn, then tried to ring Peter, but he was out, then she dialled Myra's number. Her sister's breathless voice came on to the line.

'Hello?'

'Hello, Myra.'

'Oh, hello, Jill, it's you,' said Myra. 'What's up?'

'Oh, well . . . there's the news about Sharon Bell, but that isn't why I'm ringing.' She had forgotten that Myra didn't know about Sharon.

'What about Sharon Bell? She's that nurse Mother used to work with . . . the one who gave evidence against her, isn't she?'

'That's right,' Jill said. 'Peter went to see her and found her unconscious. She'd taken sleeping pills.'

'Peter found her!' Myra gasped.

'What was he doing visiting that girl?'

'He's been seeing her for a bit. He thought he'd get her to tell the truth about Mum, but she's tried to commit suicide. She's sent Mum a letter, too.'

'I can't believe it!' Myra exclaimed. 'How stupid can Peter get! You've all gone mad! Just when everything was quietening down, it will all be raked up again. Everybody will be talking.'

'You haven't even asked after the girl!' Jill cried. 'Myra, you . . . you . . . '

'I was going to ask. How is she?'

'Pulling round.'

'They always do,' Myra said, 'people like that. They do it for sympathy and to draw attention to themselves. Trust our Peter to get mixed up in that sort of thing. Anyway, it's not so bad if she's recovering OK. What else did you want to tell me?'

'Mum's coming home,' Jill said, controlling her temper with an effort. 'The day after tomorrow.'

'Oh well, I expect she's had a good time. No doubt she'll be flaunting her suntan. It should be better than the one she showed us last time she was away. Look, I've got to go, Jill. It's nearly time for ballet school for Wendy, and I have to take Paul along too.'

The phone went dead, and as Jill replaced the receiver, her anger at her sister almost overflowed. How cutting Myra could be at times! She had always been forthright in her manner, but she was becoming a great deal worse these days, and she seemed to be drawing herself away from her family.

It must be weeks and weeks since she'd called in merely for the sake of making a visit.

Jill resolved to have a word with Peter about this. She hoped her mother's holiday had done her a lot of good, but she didn't want any setbacks because of Myra.

* * *

Peter had been feeling off colour all day. He had brought his desk work up to date, then he had made a second call on a local house with a few queries which had still to be ironed out.

On returning to the office, he finished his report with his eye on the clock. If only the time would pass so that he could go and see Sharon. He knew that he would have no peace until he saw her with even the smallest touch of life in her again. He wanted to see her open her eyes and to see her lips move.

At last he reached the end of his working day and left the office, making his way to the hospital, his stomach muscles tightening with nerves. Soon he was mingling with the other visitors as they made their way to the wards.

His arms were full of flowers and fruit, but when he reached the wards and asked for Sharon, he was not allowed to see her.

'She's still not allowed visitors,' the nurse told him.

'I . . . I see,' Peter said. 'She is better, though?' he asked anxiously. 'I mean

. . . she's pulling through all right, isn't she?'

'She is improving,' the nurse told him.

'Could you give her these flowers and the fruit? Oh, and I'll write a message for her.' Hastily he scribbled a note. 'If she needs anything — anything at all, I — I'll do my best to get it for her,' he said earnestly. 'Here's my telephone number. If she wants to see me, I'll come at once.'

'Thank you, Mr Cameron. I'll attend to it.'

The nurse smiled and Peter made his way to the stairs once more. He was empty handed, but his heart felt strangely empty as well. What could he do now?

His thoughts turned to Elizabeth and rather nervously Peter went to the bus stop and waited for a bus to take him to her flat.

Elizabeth looked cool and composed when she opened the door, but she smiled when she saw him on the doorstep.

'Hello, Peter. I was wondering when you would call again.'

'Hello, Elizabeth,' he said awkwardly. 'May I come in? I — I've been meaning to ring, but — well — things have been difficult.'

'I know,' she said quietly. 'I've heard.'

'How?' he asked.

'As a matter of fact, I wondered if you were free tonight, so I rang Jill. She told me about Sharon.'

'Oh — oh, I see,' Peter said.

He looked so tired that Elizabeth longed to put her arms round him, but something in Peter's attitude stayed her.

'You did warn me,' he said at length, 'but I wouldn't listen. Now I've as good as put Sharon in hospital. I nearly killed her.'

'Now, don't say that, Peter,' she said sharply. 'Sharon isn't your responsibility. It's true that I did warn you, though, to keep out of things like that. It's always better not to go stirring up trouble.'

'Sometimes things have to be stirred up in order to get them straightened out,' he said. 'That's what I felt anyway. Maybe I was wrong.'

'Yes, I think you were,' Elizabeth said. 'You should forget all about it now, Peter.'

'Forget!' he cried. 'How could I ever forget finding Sharon like that? And tonight, they wouldn't even let me see her. Maybe I'll see her tomorrow night.'

'No, Peter,' Elizabeth said, 'not tomorrow night, surely. We're going to a concert, remember? You'll feel much better if you go — it'll cheer you up. I mean, there are people who will be able to look after Sharon Bell and know how to handle her. You're far better to keep out of it. Why should you go running to the hospital?' she asked him.

He stared at her. She had no real notion how he felt at all, he thought. Life couldn't possibly be normal until he had seen Sharon again and if only she would smile at him, his whole life would warm into sunshine once more.

'I'm sorry about the concert, Elizabeth,'

he said contritely. 'Please try to understand.'

Peter lost no time in going home, and
his own home had never looked more
attractive to him.

★　★　★

Hugh placed a folder of notes on
Janet's desk then turned to hang up his
coat.

'One more job,' he said, 'not large,
but the ordinary work keeps coming in
fairly steadily. Any mail?'

'Nothing much, Hugh,' she said
quietly, and her voice was so subdued
that he turned to look at her closely.

'Is everything OK, Janet?'

'Oh, there is another message, Hugh.
Jill telephoned. Anna . . . Anna has
returned to London with her aunt. Jill's
written down the train times and she
says she told her mother you would
pick her up in Carlisle.'

'That's splendid,' Hugh said. 'I said I
would make time to do that. What's up,

Janet? Does it conflict with another appointment?'

'Oh no, Hugh, you'll manage Carlisle OK, it's just that . . . Hugh, I've been thinking . . . it's going to make a difference, Anna coming home, I mean.'

'In what way?' he asked.

'I've got to go away from here, Hugh,' she said huskily. 'I can't stay here every day, so close to you and . . . and having to meet Anna's eyes. I must hand in my notice.'

'Oh, Janet, I *am* sorry,' he said. 'I know how you feel and — and it's all my fault.'

'Don't say that, Hugh,' she answered quickly. 'I'm a big girl now. I knew what I was doing. I shan't leave you in the lurch, though. We'll surely be able to find a good replacement and I'll stay to teach the newcomer the ropes before I go. At least your office work won't suffer.'

On the morning he had to leave for Carlisle, Hugh rose early.

'Is there any post for me?' he asked as

he walked into the kitchen.

'I think they're all bills. Oh, except for this one.' She picked up an envelope. 'It went to the office, but Janet brought it across — she said you ought to see it right away.'

Hugh took the envelope, recognising the logo of the supermarket development company. His fingers trembled a little as he slit it open and began to read, his eyes quickly picking out the relevant details:

. . . do not wish to proceed with this project at this moment in time . . . if decision is reversed at a future date, we will be pleased to contact you . . . detailed estimate will be returned to you under separate cover . . .

With shaking hands Hugh put the letter back into the envelope. His disappointment was like a physical pain. He saw Jill looking at him with concern and he managed a quick smile.

'I'd better not start to add up these bills,' he said ruefully, 'or I'll never be able to afford the petrol to get me to Carlisle. I'll go now, dear. Don't forget the reception committee for your mother. She loves that sort of thing.' He smiled and held out his hands.

'I won't, Dad,' she said, giving him a hug. 'Somehow I feel that everything is going to be all right now.'

Hugh nodded, wishing with all his heart that he could share those feelings of Jill's.

★   ★   ★

Waiting on the platform at Carlisle Station, Hugh turned his coat collar up against a surprisingly chilly wind, but soon the train was sliding into the station.

Hugh had to look twice at the beautiful woman who descended from the train before he was sure it was his wife. Her lovely hair had been set in a new style and Aunt Helen had insisted upon buying her a new velvet suit in a soft shade of cinnamon in thanks for all the help Anna had given her. It suited her glowing beauty to perfection. Her skin had been warmed by the sun to a rich apricot and her eyes sparkled with light.

Slowly he walked forward as Anna hurried towards him, then he was holding her in his arms and kissing her briefly. She wore a faint elusive perfume which had been a parting gift from Alan Haydon, and Hugh suddenly felt shy of her — afraid that his neglect of her over recent months had driven her too far away from him.

'Oh, Hugh, it's lovely to be home, or almost home.' She laughed breathlessly.

'Yes,' he agreed lamely. 'Anna — I — you look beautiful and I'm so glad to see you. The car's on the other side of the station,' he said, 'over the bridge. Do you want anything to eat?'

'I had a meal on the train,' she said. 'Are you really glad to see me Hugh?'

'Of course,' he said quickly.

How wonderful it would have been to

be able to tell her that he had landed a contract which would have made them financially comfortable for some years to come . . .

In the car, Anna curbed her desire to ask a thousand questions while Hugh negotiated the one-way traffic system before heading north for Castleden.

'I've so much to tell you, Hugh . . . I hardly know where to begin,' she said, 'but first of all, I want to know all that's been happening at home. How is everybody?'

'Oh . . . fine,' he said brightly. 'Everything is grand. The family are all looking forward to your arrival.'

Anna glanced at him sideways and saw how Hugh's hands were gripping the steering wheel. Something between them wasn't quite right, yet there had been that old flash of admiration and — and surely love for her when their eyes first met.

When she came to ask about Peter he hesitated before answering.

'He's been going to see Sharon Bell,'

Hugh said rather thoughtlessly.

'Sharon Bell?' she echoed. 'What on earth for?'

'I — well — I think he met her again, though I'm vague about the details, and they've become friends. She . . . she's in hospital at the moment. He goes to see her.'

'Oh, poor Sharon. That's rather different,' Anna said sympathetically. 'I'm glad Peter's doing that for her. You know, when we first worked together, I became very fond of her. I thought she was a really nice girl. That's why . . . ' Her voice tailed off. That was why she had found it difficult to believe that Sharon had not supported her.

'It's all in the past,' she said, rather sadly, 'I think we ought to look forward to the future, Hugh, don't you?'

'Why not?' he replied heartily.

Jill had checked up on the house many times and had assured herself that every speck of dust had been whisked away, and that the casserole she had prepared was not drying up in the oven.

She had telephoned Myra and practically forced her into promising to come round and welcome their mother home.

'You're full of excuses, Myra,' Jill said, having already decided that she was going to make her point. 'We don't want to see our family splitting up like this. I think you ought to make more time for Mum, so just you come round tonight, even for a little while.'

'It will have to be a little while then,' said Myra grudgingly, 'but OK. I may be a bit late, though.'

'I mean all of you,' Jill insisted.

'No, the children have to go to bed and Charles will have to sit in. We just can't get baby-sitters these days.'

'No doubt you miss Mum for that!'

'So I'll call in later,' Myra said, ignoring the interruption.

'We'll expect you,' Jill said crisply.

★   ★   ★

Adrian arrived first and admired the tea table.

He turned to grin at her, then would have taken her in his arms had not Peter walked in the door and hurried forward to spread out his hands in front of the fire.

'You'll have to take it easy, Peter,' Adrian warned. 'You look wound up.'

'I'm OK,' Peter said, 'just a wee bit cold, that's all. What time are we expecting Mum and Dad?'

'Any time now,' Jill told him.

It was a quarter of an hour later when the car drew up at the door and Anna was once again home in the midst of her family who made no attempt to conceal their delight.

'Mum, you look fabulous,' Jill enthused.

'Well, thank you,' Anna replied. 'I've brought you all presents and some special ones for Wendy and Paul.'

'Myra's coming round later,' said Jill quickly, 'but we won't hold supper for her. I think we ought to eat now or that casserole will be fed up having me staring at it every five minutes. It'll be ruined by now.' She smiled ruefully at Anna.

'Don't believe her, Mrs Cameron.' Adrian laughed. 'She's becoming an excellent cook.'

'And a fine housewife,' Anna said, looking round. She caught the shy glance which Jill exchanged with Adrian and again her heart warmed. She could not wish for anything better for Jill.

But Peter? Her eyes went to her only son whom she loved so very deeply. He wasn't his usual cheerful self. She was going to have to ask him about Sharon Bell, but not until after tea.

It was an excellent meal and there was a great deal of laughter as Anna told her family small anecdotes about her holiday.

★   ★   ★

'What was that man Alan Haydon like?' Jill asked. 'Aunt Helen kept mentioning him.'

Anna's cheeks warmed. 'He's an American and very charming. He's getting over his wife's death. I hope the holiday helped him as much as it helped me.'

There was a short silence then Jill glanced at Peter meaningfully and turned to her mother.

'There are a few letters for you, Mum,' she said. 'There's one specially . . . ' She looked again at Peter. 'Maybe we ought to tell you a little about it first.'

'What about it?' Anna asked, and again there was silence as her family all looked at her awkwardly.

'Peter thinks it's from Sharon Bell, dear,' said Hugh, and put his hand over Anna's. 'Perhaps we ought to tell you that she's in hospital because of an — an overdose of sleeping pills.'

Anna's mouth fell open.

'Sleeping pills!' She stared at Peter. 'You mean, she tried to . . . to kill herself?'

'It was all my fault,' Peter said miserably.

Jill had pulled up chairs to the fireside and they all sat round the fire. Adrian would have excused himself, but Jill insisted that he stayed, and Peter, too, asked him not to leave.

'You've been in this right from the start, Adrian,' he said.

Awkwardly and rather painfully Peter began to tell Anna about how he had sought out Sharon once again.

'But why, Peter?' she asked.

'Because — well — because I wasn't satisfied that she told the truth at the trial. I wanted her to admit that much. It was making such a difference to us as a family . . .'

Anna's clear eyes were regarding him steadily.

'I kept on at her,' Peter said miserably, 'even when I knew she was upset because her engagement had been broken. Then . . . Then I found her unconscious in her flat with the empty bottle beside her. I got her to hospital, Mum, but . . . but it was touch and go.'

'Oh, Peter,' Anna said, her voice warm with sympathy.

'She's sent you a letter. I recognised her handwriting, and that's why we felt . . . ' He looked at Jill and Adrian. ' . . . we felt that I had to tell you before you opened it.'

'Then by all means let's read the letter,' Anna said.

'I'll get it,' Jill said, rising to her feet.

A moment later Anna was laying aside her other letters and selecting the one from Sharon. Before she could open it, the back door banged shut and Myra sailed in breezily.

'Hello, Mum,' she said, bending to give her a peck on the cheek. 'Goodness, but aren't we smart? That perfume must have cost a fortune! Aren't you lucky you can afford it?'

'Sit down, Myra,' Anna said quietly. 'What I can and cannot afford is my own affair. Are Charles and the children well? I'm looking forward to seeing them again.'

'Oh, they're fine,' said Myra. 'Have I

interrupted something?'

'I was going to read a letter from Sharon Bell — '

'That girl again!'

'Be quiet, Myra,' Jill said in a low controlled voice. 'This letter is important.'

' . . . A Slip Of The Tongue'

Easing the letter gently out of its envelope, Anna was aware of everyone's eyes upon her and she began to read out loud. Sharon didn't try to find excuses for herself. She told Anna about Derek McIver's part in the affair and how he asked her to put aside Anna's request for her to go on duty early that fateful day.

I shouldn't have allowed myself to be persuaded, Sharon wrote. *It wasn't Derek's fault, but mine. I'm so ashamed that I cannot live with it. Not only did I let you down, but I allowed old Mrs Foster to die. I was a coward, afraid to admit what I had done when the police questioned me. Instead, I let you take the blame.*

But now Peter has made me realise how awful it has been for you and your family. I don't know how to put things right. I'm so unhappy about what has happened, and I've decided to write it all down, then perhaps your name will be cleared.

But I can't go through what you went through, Mrs Cameron. I couldn't face that . . .

The writing tailed off and there was heavy silence in the room before Peter spoke.

'If only I'd left things alone. I must have put her through some sort of hell . . . '

'Poor lass,' Anna said softly. 'She's certainly been troubled in her mind . . . '

Myra had pulled her chair forward, hardly listening to what the others were saying.

'Can I see the letter, Mum?' she asked, an almost feverish light in her eyes. She held out her hand for the letter.

Anna passed it over and Myra scanned it avidly. It was true. It was a confession, properly signed and all down in black and white.

'You'll take it to the police, of course, Mum,' she said, her eyes shining. 'They'll see to it that your name is cleared.'

'If you do that,' Adrian said quietly, 'then Sharon Bell will probably have to serve a jail sentence after all. Apart from anything else she has committed perjury.'

'Why should we care about her?' Myra asked, rounding on him.

'Because she's a sick girl!' Peter cried. 'You forget that she wrote this when she decided to take her own life.'

'What difference does that make?' Myra asked.

'If you can't see the difference, I'm sorry for you, Myra,' Peter said tightly. 'I don't know what's got into you these days.'

Anna had retrieved her letter.

'There is no need for any argument,' she said, her voice quiet but authoritative. 'This letter will never be made public. What's done is done and there's no point in raking it all up again. It *was* my fault, whatever Sharon believes, and I shouldn't have put such responsibility on to a young girl.'

'But, Mum!' Myra cried. 'Don't you see —'

'No, Myra,' Anna said firmly. 'It's my decision, dear. No-one must know of this but ourselves. Sharon has suffered enough.'

★   ★   ★

The following evening Peter arrived early at the hospital and was delighted to be given permission to see Sharon.

'Hello, Sharon,' he said, leaning forward. 'I'm so glad you're better. I've been here every day asking for you.'

'I don't want you even to look at me,' she said. 'Can't you understand what I did? Did — did your mother get my letter?'

'Yes, she did, and she says it's all in the past. She's going to come to see you . . . ' Peter felt a touch of fear when he saw how white and ill she looked. If

Sharon felt that her life was so hopeless, how was she ever going to fight back to normal health?

Almost without thinking he rose to his feet and bent over her, kissing her cold lips.

'Sharon . . . darling . . . this won't do,' he said urgently. 'You've got to put it behind you and start to fight back, for my sake as well as your own. Can't you see that?'

Her eyes widened again and she stared at him, then he saw large tears forming in her eyes and great sobs began to shake her shoulders. Peter stood back almost helplessly, then looked around as a nurse hurried forward.

'She's better to get this out,' she said to Peter as the girl's body was racked with sobs. 'You'd better go, but I think she'll begin to make progress now.'

'I'll be back, darling,' Peter said, touching Sharon's soft hair. 'Just try to get better, that's all.'

Going home in the bus, Peter's heart

felt easier as he thought over his visit to Sharon, and his words to her seemed to echo in his mind. He wanted Sharon better for his sake. He knew now that he loved Sharon Bell and wanted her always in his life.

But how would his family react to that?

★   ★   ★

Anna had been tired on her first evening at home and had automatically gone back to her small bedroom, but the following day she had considered the matter carefully, and after breakfast she decided to move her personal belongings back into her old bedroom.

The house was busy that day with Myra bringing the children for a visit and Anna sorting out her luggage and giving everyone the presents she had brought back from Greece.

She found time to send flowers to Sharon, then she went upstairs to move all her personal things back into the main bedroom.

She was still busy with her task when Hugh arrived home and walked upstairs to the bedroom. Slowly Anna rose from a kneeling position beside the chest of drawers.

'I've moved back in here, Hugh,' she said, her eyes wide and questioning. 'I — I hope you don't mind.'

'Mind!' Hugh's eyes were alight as he took her in his arms, then suddenly the image of Janet was before him and he stiffened a little. His heart felt sick as he held his wife to him. If only it had never happened, how happy he would be at this moment.

Ever sensitive to his feelings, Anna looked up at him.

'Hugh?' she asked, with a hint of uncertainty.

'Of course I don't mind,' he said roughly, and kissed her.

That evening Anna wore an attractive new nightdress she had bought on holiday and was already in bed when Hugh came out of the bathroom. He stood so long in the middle of the bedroom floor that she looked at him with concern. Things were still not quite right between them.

'Is there anything wrong, Hugh?' she asked.

Quietly he sat down on the bed and took her hands.

'There's something I must tell you, Anna,' he said. His mouth felt dry and he swallowed painfully. He had come to realise that, sooner or later, he would have to tell Anna about Janet Fairbairn, but now that the moment had come, he could hardly find the words.

'I think you'd better tell me, Hugh,' Anna said eventually. 'Have — have you not been well?'

'Oh, it's nothing like that,' he assured her. 'It — it's Janet.'

'Janet! Janet Fairbairn?'

Hugh nodded, then again met her eyes as he began to tell her about the night he had stayed at Janet's flat.

'We were so tired after all that work, and with the supermarket deal now being held in the balance, it might have been for nothing — '

'Nothing! You call that nothing!'

'No, Anna! Of course not. I mean the *work* might all have been for nothing. With Janet — well — it just happened. I can't explain more than that. You seemed to be so far away from me, in another world. It was as though I was living in a dream.'

Anna had thrown back the bed-clothes and was wandering aimlessly round the bedroom. She listened to Hugh's words, but they hardly made any sense to her.

She only knew that the moment she had turned her back, he had gone to Janet Fairbairn. It had only happened once, he assured her over and over, and Janet was leaving her job because of it. She was going out of their lives. But it was a betrayal . . .

'Do you love her?' Anna asked harshly.

'Oh, Anna,' Hugh replied, 'do you really have to ask that? You must know that you have always had my love, and always will. I do love Janet in a way, but only as a dear friend. I'm not ashamed of that. It would never have happened except for the circumstances. It really seemed like a dream.'

A dream, thought Anna, as she idly played with the jars on her dressing-table. Suddenly she was aware of the subtle expensive perfume which clung to her fingers. A dream! She had lived a dream on board ship, one evening as she danced in Alan Haydon's arms. How long ago that seemed!

She had allowed Alan to kiss her and had basked in his undoubted admiration. She had also come very close to going into Alan's cabin that night. How could she judge Hugh when her own conduct might have been just as reprehensible! She had found that extra bit of strength to say, 'No,' but how easily she might have given in.

'Anna?' Hugh's voice was low, but full of appeal.

Slowly she turned round and her heart melted when she saw his white face and anxious eyes.

'It's OK, Hugh,' she said gently. 'You don't have to explain any more. I — I just had to come to terms with it all. I'm just very glad that it wasn't your health that was the problem. We can live with — anything else.'

Hugh swept his wife into his arms.

'Oh, Anna, my darling,' he said, 'I never hoped — I never believed you could accept it without making me feel I couldn't live with myself.'

'There will be none of that,' Anna said sharply. 'I spent far too long feeling ashamed and not wanting to live with myself. Now that's all behind me, and has been put firmly into the past. I shan't forget, and I don't want to forget. It makes the present so much more precious. We mustn't destroy our love.'

'Then you still love me?' he asked.

'I still love you, Hugh.'

*　*　*

Anna was concerned for Peter when she saw how badly he had been affected by

Sharon's attempt to take her own life. She knew her son was sleeping badly and she was careful to prepare light nourishing meals in an effort to coax him to eat.

Anna pondered over whether she ought to go and see Sharon, then decided to ring the hospital and inquire after her.

'She's resting after treatment,' a nurse told her after she had been put through to the ward.

'But is she any better?' Anna pursued.

'She's responding to treatment and is comfortable.'

'Thank you.' Anna sighed, putting down the telephone. It would take time before Sharon was well again.

As she turned to go into the sitting-room the ringing of the doorbell startled her, and she walked quickly to the door, her eyes widening when she recognised Stephen Foster and his wife, Doreen.

'Would it be possible for us to talk to

you, Mrs Cameron?' he said gravely.

'Please come in,' she invited warily. 'I was just going to make some coffee. Will you join me?'

'I'd love a cup of coffee,' Doreen Foster said, and smiled.

Anna had to conceal her surprise. Mrs Foster had always been cool and reserved towards her. Quickly she made the coffee and carried it through to the sitting-room.

'I understand you've just had a splendid holiday in the Greek Islands,' said Mrs Foster, as she accepted a small savoury biscuit.

'Quite right, but how — '

'Oh, Charles and Myra had dinner with us last night,' said Stephen Foster easily. 'As a matter of fact, Mrs Cameron, that's why we are here. We wish to apologise to you.'

'Whatever for?' Anna asked.

'For believing that you really were so neglectful of my mother when we knew she was so fond of you, and used to sing your praises to the sky. Somehow it always seemed like a betrayal, the way you left her that day, and when you appeared to be making excuses, it was even worse.

'We were deeply angered, Doreen and I, but we should have known my mother had better judgement than that, and that the young girl who gave evidence could have been lying.'

Anna's face had grown white, but now slow anger began to boil in her.

'Myra told you,' she said in a voice she could scarcely control. 'How dare she! I'm sorry, Mrs Foster, but Sharon Bell's confession was confidential and I made my wishes very clear to my family, that it must go no further than the four walls of this house. I am very angry with Myra!' Her voice echoed her fury.

'Oh, don't be hard on her,' said Stephen Foster. 'I'm afraid she had told Charles, as any wife would tell her husband, and he dropped a hint of it quite by accident. Myra pleaded with us to forget it.'

'I'm sure she did!' Anna said in the same hard voice. She knew her daughter very well. Trust Myra to give the information to the Fosters somehow!

'She told us it was confidential, but Doreen and I are very glad we have been told. It's this ring, you see.'

Stephen Foster reached into his pocket and brought out the beautiful solitaire ring which old Mrs Foster had given to Anna.

Seeing it again brought a sudden rush of tears to Anna's eyes and she tried to blink them away.

'I — I'm sorry,' she whispered, reaching into her pocket for her handkerchief. 'It always makes me think of your mother.'

'I know,' Stephen said. 'That's just it! Every time Doreen and I look at it, it seems to remind us that we have no right to keep it. Deep down I've always known that my mother gave it to you. Doreen has her own jewellery, and would never wear this ring.'

'It never felt like mine,' Mrs Foster said.

'Please accept it, Mrs Cameron,' Stephen Foster said earnestly. 'I know you don't want to make the letter public and I respect you for that. As much as anything that tells me that my mother was not wrong about you. This ring is yours, not ours, and I want you to take it back.'

Anna had been shaking her head, but now her eyes went to the ring once again. It was very pretty. She knew, now, that it was also very valuable, but its true value lay in the fact that it symbolised the love and affection she and old Mrs Foster had had for one another.

Slowly she held out her hand and Stephen Foster put the box on her palm and closed her fingers round it.

'Thank you,' she said huskily, unable to say more for the lump in her throat.

'May you have long health to enjoy it,' he said gently, and Mrs Foster bent to kiss her cheek.

* ★ ★

At that moment, Jill and Adrian were strolling along the river-bank. He was now awaiting final confirmation that his future was assured.

'I'm restless while I wait,' he confessed. 'I need you with me, Jill. Let's go walking as usual, along by the river.'

They said little until they left the footpath and turned off along a narrow path which skirted the riverbank, then Adrian clasped Jill's hand and held it firmly in his own.

'Have you thought any more about your future, Jill?' he asked.

'I've thought about it a great deal, Adrian,' she confessed.

'And?' he prompted.

'I'll never make a doctor. It isn't really in me, though I'm deeply interested in medicine. But I'd be perfectly content with a seat in the wings.'

'A seat in the wings!' He looked

264

puzzled then her meaning became clear. 'Will you really marry me, Jill? I do love you, my darling.'

'And I love you, Adrian. I don't think I knew how much until recently, but all I want from life is to be your wife.'

'Oh, Jill.' Adrian swept her into his arms and kissed her, and Jill's heart sang with happiness.

'Do you think your grandfather will be pleased, Adrian?'

'He'll be impressed by how sensible I am,' Adrian said, grinning. 'He has great respect for the Cameron ladies.'

'We'll go home and tell Mum and Dad,' said Jill. 'They're so full of themselves these days that they hardly notice me. Thank goodness I've got someone of my own or I would feel neglected.'

'Well, I shan't neglect you,' Adrian promised. 'We must choose an engagement ring, darling.'

'Time enough for that,' Jill said. 'Let's stun them with our surprise news first of all.'

Peter was out when Jill and Adrian hurried home to tell her parents their news. He had eaten a hurried tea with Anna encouraging him to try small samples of the type of cookery which she, herself, had eaten on board ship.

'I just want your opinion, Peter,' she said. 'Try a tiny piece.'

Everything tasted like sawdust to Peter, but he ate the helpings obediently and complimented his mother on her cooking. Then he grabbed his coat and ran for the bus which would take him to the hospital in time for the start of visiting hour.

Sharon was now sitting up in bed, though her face was very pale and her eyes heavily shadowed as Peter approached her bed and put down a basketful of fruit.

'Hello, Sharon,' he said, his eyes taking in every detail of her face.

'Hello.' She looked at the fruit and shook her head. 'You shouldn't, Peter! I'll never eat all you've brought for me. Your — your mother has sent me flowers. I didn't know what to say when I saw them. I've had to ask the nurse to put them over on another table. They make me so ashamed.'

'Oh, Sharon!' Peter exclaimed, as he sat down beside her bed. 'You mustn't say things like that. It's all over now. You're getting better and we must think about the future.'

'What future?' she said tiredly.

Peter looked at her pale face as she turned her head away. Once again the soft hair curls lay on her forehead, giving her a childish look. She had lost a great deal of weight and the bones of her face stood out clearly, giving her a look of delicate beauty which caught at his heart. He reached out to take her hand.

'I'm talking about our future, Sharon,' he said softly.

Her eyes flew open.

'What do you mean, our future, Peter?'

He swallowed nervously. Was it wise to tell her how he felt? But already he was committed.

'I'm in love with you, Sharon,' he said quietly. 'I want to marry you. I don't want to ever lose sight of you again.'

Sharon's eyes were wide as she looked at Peter. He had come into her life, filling her with resentment at his probing of things she had wanted to forget. But even now she knew that he had been a friend to her by exposing the old wounds which were poisoning her soul. Yes, she had a lot to be grateful for.

He bent forward and kissed her cold lips, made salty by her tears.

'That was a salty kiss,' he said. 'The next one will be sweeter. Better get used to me, Sharon darling. I intend to be around for a long time.'

★　★　★

Jill and Adrian's news was like balm to Anna's heart, and she and Hugh congratulated the young couple, and were glad that they intended to be sensible and wait until Adrian was settled into his first post before they married.

'I'll find something to do meantime,' Jill said happily. 'Let me know if you hear of something, Daddy.'

'I might just do that, Jill.' Hugh said thoughtfully.

Anna had shown him the ring and told him about the visit from the Fosters.

'It's nice to have the ring back,' she admitted. 'But I was very angry with Myra, and this time she's not going to get off with it. She's taken a high-handed attitude with me quite a few times, but this is once too often.'

The following afternoon, Anna walked round to Myra's house, turning towards the back door as she had so often done in the past.

'Hello, Mother,' Myra said as she appeared at the kitchen door. 'I didn't hear you come in.'

'I expect you know why I've come,'

Anna said evenly. 'I've had a visit from Mr and Mrs Foster.'

'Then they came to see you!' Myra said, smiling. 'I'm so pleased.'

'Well, I'm not at all pleased!' Anna said in a low, controlled voice. 'I told all of you my wishes with regard to Sharon Bell's confession, and you all gave your word not to repeat it out of the family. It didn't take you long to break it, Myra, since it suited you to do so — '

'It was just a slip of the tongue!' Myra cried.

Little Wendy was tugging at her skirt.

'Can we have one of your sweeties, Mummy?' she asked. 'One for Paul and one for me.'

'Help yourself,' Myra said tonelessly.

'One of the big ones, Mummy — instead of our little ones?'

'I said yes,' Myra said irritably. 'It was only a slip of the tongue, Mother.'

'Your tongue has been slipping fairly often in recent months,' Anna said. 'You might as well know that I've had as much as I want to take from you!'

'I'm sorry that what Charles said has upset you, Mother,' Myra said, 'but I'm not apologising. I think that Mr and Mrs Foster had to know.'

'To suit you, of course,' Anna said. 'Myra, I'm disappointed in you. Even now you want to put yourself first.'

Wendy had taken Paul through to the sitting-room, then suddenly her mother and grandmother were startled by her loud screaming.

'Mummy! Mummy! It's Paul! He's choking on his sweetie. He can't breathe . . . '

True Love

Myra rushed through to the sitting-room, closely followed by her mother as Wendy continued to scream.

Little Paul was making queer rasping noises, his eyes staring and his face convulsed as he fought for breath, and Myra also cried out in fear. The power seemed to leave her body as she reached out for Paul, but her mother was there before her, turning him round and giving him a smart rap on the back of the neck.

The dislodged sweet flew out of his mouth and Anna forced him to breathe, then dealt with his sickness and encouraged his loud roars, when his breathing returned to normal.

Myra was holding Wendy, both of them sobbing quietly, then she turned to her mother.

'Oh, Mum,' she whispered. 'If you

hadn't been here — '

'If I hadn't been here, it might not have happened,' Anna said briskly. 'You wouldn't have allowed him to eat hard sweets which are far too big to put in his mouth.'

'I — I just forgot for a moment.'

Hugging Paul to her, Myra was realising how desperately she wanted to protect her child.

How easy it was to make a mistake! Was this how her mother had felt that day she left Mrs Foster and ran home to attend to Jill? Had she been just as afraid for Jill as she herself now was for Paul?

Myra's tears began to flow faster than ever.

'Oh, Mum,' she said, 'I — I've been horrible to you. I could only think of myself and my family. I couldn't see it from your point of view, or Jill's for that matter. She was really very ill that day. You must have been so anxious about her, yet — yet I've never understood until now . . . '

Anna's eyes misted with tears. She had shed so many because of Myra's attitude, but these were tears of thanksgiving. A sore had been healed in her heart. The Myra who looked at her now was the daughter she had loved all her life, and who had loved her.

'It's all behind us now, Myra,' she said. 'We'll make a new beginning, my dear. Here, let's tidy this place up and we'll have a cup of tea together. Paul will be fine now.'

* * *

Peter was home later than usual that evening and Jill was about to go up to bed when he rushed into the sitting-room and warmed his hands by the fire.

'It's raining cats and dogs,' he announced.

'Sit here,' Jill said, pulling up her chair. 'I'm just going up to bed.'

'No, stay for a minute,' Peter said. 'I want to talk to Mum and Dad, and perhaps it also concerns you, too, Jill. I mean, it concerns all of us in this house.'

Anna and Hugh exchanged glances.

'What's all this about, Peter?' Hugh asked.

'It's about Sharon Bell,' Peter began. 'Sharon's due out of hospital on Saturday and she just can't look after herself, Mum. I'd like to bring her home here for a few days.'

Anna was staring at him levelly as he tried to explain.

'I mean, she can't go back to that empty flat,' he went on.

'Hasn't she got relatives, Peter?' Anna asked quietly.

'Only an aunt and uncle and they have their own family to worry about. Sharon has been standing on her own feet since she took up nursing.'

'That's right. I remember now,' Anna said, her heart touched by the girl's lack of a supportive family.

'It would only be for a few days, until I can make other arrangements when we see how well she is,' Peter added.

'You!' Jill cried. 'Why you? Why should you make yourself responsible for Sharon Bell?'

'I'm in love with Sharon,' he said quietly. 'I want to marry her one day.'

'In *love* with her!' Jill exclaimed. 'That's just ridiculous, Peter. Not long ago you were mooning over Elizabeth Caldwell. What's happened to her?'

'I wasn't truly in love with Elizabeth,' Peter said, 'though I liked her a great deal, but I never felt the same way about her as I do about Sharon, and she didn't feel that way about me. I had a letter the other day from her in Edinburgh.

'She's gone back to living with her family there, now that she's been promoted in her job. She wants me to bring Sharon to Edinburgh one day soon and we'll make a foursome date with Elizabeth's new boyfriend.'

'You seem to be wandering off the point as usual, Peter,' his father said rather heavily.

'Sorry, Dad, but I didn't mean to

276

wander off the point. I'd like the permission of all of you to bring Sharon Bell home and for her to get to know my family. I've asked her to marry me, but she's turned me down, though I don't accept that so easily. She just needs to get to know us all a bit better and — and to know that we don't hold it against her . . . What she did at the trial, I mean.'

'You must be out of your tiny mind,' Jill said. 'Have Sharon Bell living with us! Asking Mum to accept her as a daughter one day . . . my sister-in-law . . . after what she did! You're crazy, Peter!'

He stared at her, his face pale and set.

'She's been punished enough, Jill,' he said quietly. 'As it is, I'm going to need Mum's help in trying to persuade her to come, but I know Mum will help. If anyone can put Sharon back to good health, both mentally and physically, then it's Mum. I mean, we all have each other, and you have Adrian, Jill, but

Sharon doesn't have anybody.'

Jill bit her lip. Adrian had passed his examinations with flying colours and nothing now stood in the way of their future happiness. She wanted to talk to her mother about her wedding plans, but had had no opportunity to do so yet.

Jill glanced at her mother, seeing that Anna was regarding her anxiously.

'Well,' she said, rising to her feet, 'I'm off to bed. It's up to Mum and Dad as to whether or not they want to welcome Sharon, Peter. As far as I'm concerned, it's OK. I'm sorry I flew off at you, but I'll be nice to her. I'll do my best for you.'

Peter's eyes shone.

'Thanks, Jill. I knew I could count on you.' He turned to his mother. 'Mum?'

'You go to bed, too, Peter,' said his father. 'Your mother and I want a little talk on our own before we decide.'

⋆   ⋆   ⋆

'Well?' Hugh asked, after they'd gone. 'That's a turn-up. How do you feel about it, Anna?'

'My first instincts are to say yes immediately because I do feel sorry for Sharon, but that would be ill-considered,' Anna said. 'I've often landed myself in trouble by wanting to make the generous gesture, but this time it's much more serious.

'This time it is Peter's life — his future happiness. We've got to get it right, Hugh. He says he'll need me to persuade Sharon and that means that she isn't sure yet, even if Peter is. But I can persuade her whole-heartedly or half-heartedly. I've got to know how I really feel before I go to see her.'

Hugh nodded, staring into the fire.

'I wonder if he is truly in love with her?' he mused.

'Don't you know?' Anna asked softly. 'Can't you recognise true love, Hugh?'

He looked across at her and smiled, then reached over to take her hand and draw her into his arms.

'It's the most wonderful gift a man can have, darling,' he said. 'We've found that out. Ours has taken a few knocks, but they've only served to keep it shining even brighter. I can see that Peter and Sharon wouldn't have it very easy either, but if their love is like ours, they'll have something really worthwhile.'

Anna leaned her head on his shoulder.

'I'll do what I can for Peter,' she said. 'Sharon can come and see how she likes being part of our family. If she's happy, she and Peter will have our blessing, and if not, then they'll just have to work it out for themselves.'

'You make it sound simple,' Hugh commented.

'It isn't at all simple. We might hurt her without thinking and she might irritate us, but we'll give it a try. It's funny, but I think I'm going to enjoy it.'

'You're certainly back to normal, Anna Cameron,' Hugh said. 'Running all our lives.'

She drew breath for an indignant protest, then saw the twinkle in his eyes.

'Come on, darling let's lock up for the night,' she said, standing up. 'We've had enough for one day!'

★ ★ ★

The house was full of bustle and excitement next day after Hugh and Peter had left for work. Peter's eyes had shone with hope when his parents told him that he could bring Sharon home with their blessing.

'I'll call and see her, Peter,' Anna promised. 'I'll see to it that she knows she's welcome.'

'Thanks, Mum,' Peter said. 'I knew she would be OK here.'

It was a compliment, thought Anna, as she watched him rushing out of the gate. She should be thankful that her family was such that Peter would want to bring Sharon to them for comfort.

Jill was hovering about, and Anna could tell that her daughter also had something on her mind.

'Well?' she asked, after they had washed up together. 'Is it Peter and Sharon, or have you been writing away for a job again?'

Jill's mouth opened a little.

'How did you know? I mean, that I had something on my mind?'

'You've been scratching your eyebrows all morning. Is it Peter?'

'No, it's Adrian,' Jill said. 'You know we were going to wait before we got married, Mum. Well, we — I wondered if we couldn't get married a bit sooner, perhaps in a month or two, or — or just a few weeks. Adrian has qualified now.'

'Old Dr Scott must be so proud of him.'

'I'm proud of him, too, Mum,' Jill said. 'I know I'm still young and all that, but we're very sure, Adrian and I.'

'You want to be a doctor's wife instead of a doctor?'

'Yes — no . . . I mean, I wouldn't care what Adrian had chosen to do, I would still want to marry him. I want

Adrian, not his job, but it does help that I can take an interest in his work. Mum — couldn't we get married soon?'

Anna sighed.

'Let's think about it for a day or two, darling,' she said. 'Have you thought about what you'd like to do in the meantime?'

'Help Daddy now that Janet has gone,' Jill answered promptly. 'She got an awfully good job, you know, and Daddy couldn't stand in her way. She'll be living in London and I think she's quite thrilled about it.'

'I know,' Anna said, and turned away a little. She was glad Janet Fairbairn's life was moving into new exciting channels. She didn't blame Janet, but she had to confess she was glad Janet was going.

'Adrian wants to come and see you and Daddy again tonight,' Jill continued. 'Do you think it would be OK?'

'I don't see why not,' Anna said. 'Where are you going now?'

'Round to see Daddy,' Jill told her happily. 'Maybe I can even make a start at helping in the office. He's quite busy again now.'

'I know,' Anna said. The business was making fairly steady progress and soon, when Jill and Peter were off their hands, they would really be quite comfortably off.

'Couldn't we have a party on Saturday when Sharon arrives?' Jill asked. 'We could celebrate my engagement to Adrian, and invite old Dr Scott. I mean, Sharon knows him, too. It might make her feel welcome.'

Anna drew her younger daughter into her arms.

'Go and see your father,' she said, kissing her cheek. 'We'll talk things over tonight. Ask him about Saturday, too, but my guess is that he'll deny you nothing. I'd better start preparing for a party!'

★　★　★

Peter was glad that in a few more days he would no longer be making the bus trip to the hospital. The doctors and nursing staff had been wonderful to Sharon, but he wanted to get her away from the atmosphere of the place, and into the normal, loving warmth of his own home.

He had continued to persuade Sharon to accept his invitation, and as he walked into the ward, he saw that she was now looking much brighter and that she was even managing a smile as he walked over to the bed.

'Only two more days, Sharon,' he said, 'then I can take you home.'

'You never give up, do you, Peter?' she asked and sighed, but he detected a new note in her voice.

'No, I don't. Did Mother come to see you?'

Sharon nodded.

'She — she was very nice. She talked me into coming to your home, but I'll only come for a few days, Peter, then I'll go up to Forfar and see my Aunt Peggy and Uncle Drew. They know what happened. I'll have to try to make them understand. I'm not going to hide from anything any more, though, Peter.'

'That's my girl. You'll like it at home, truly you will. Mother is busily planning a welcome home combined with an engagement party . . . '

'Engagement party!' This time there was shock and alarm on her face.

'Oh, not for us,' Peter said rather sadly, and watched as she relaxed once more. 'It's for Jill and Adrian Scott.'

'Oh, I didn't know. I'm — I'm happy for your sister. How will she feel about me? Your other sister, too? And your father?'

'That's enough. They all want you to come. We'll cross bridges when we come to them. And, Sharon, even if you don't love me yet, you do like me, don't you?'

'I like you very much Peter,' she confessed.

'That's enough to be going on with,' he said quietly. 'As I say, I don't give up easily, but I do like to have my feet pointed in the right direction.'

Suddenly she was laughing and Peter's heart leapt. He had not heard her laughter in weeks.

'I'm bringing the car on Saturday,' he told her. 'Just be ready on time.'

Jill had spared time to put bowls of early spring flowers all round the house, and the whole place was full of warmth and laughter as Adrian arrived, with old Dr Scott, who warmly shook Anna's hand, then turned to Hugh.

'This is a happy day for me,' he said.

Myra and Charles had arrived with the children. As Anna had predicted, Myra had had plenty to say about Sharon.

'At least she's going to remember her manners and welcome Sharon today,' Anna said to Hugh with a smile.

'Of course she is,' Hugh said. 'Don't worry, darling, there's a lot of you in Myra. She just covers it up now and again.'

Peter had taken his father's car to the hospital and now Anna and Jill were rather excitedly making sure that everything was as nice as possible for the girl's arrival.

'Perhaps we shouldn't have had the party for a few days,' Jill said, suddenly nervous.

'No, I think Sharon will settle in better if there's this sort of atmosphere,' Anna said. 'She won't be so self-conscious. It was a good idea of yours, Jill.'

'Do you think she'll like my ring?' Jill asked, looking at the pretty ruby, surrounded by small diamonds.

'She'll love it, as we all do.'

'Adrian chose it.'

Anna nodded. She was hearing about Adrian's activities every five minutes at the moment. At least Jill had agreed to a summer wedding and not to rush things too much.

'He's playing tiddlywinks with the children,' Jill said, even more proudly. 'Charles and Dr Scott are setting the world to rights, and Myra is getting herself into a proper frame of mind for Sharon. In other words, the household is normal.'

The household is normal! The words echoed in Anna's head as she walked back into the sitting-room. Her heart swelled with happiness and thanksgiving as she looked round the family she loved so much. They had all been through dark days, but now they were facing the sunshine once more.

Suddenly the smooth, dark blue bonnet of Hugh's car slid to a stop at the gate and Anna turned to her husband.

'They're here, darling,' she said.

Hugh rose and together they went to the door of their home, throwing it open in welcome.

A pale, slender wraith of a girl with soft, fair, curling hair walked up the path with Peter close behind.

Anna ran down the steps and threw her arms wide.

'Welcome home, Sharon,' she said gently.

The girl's face lit up with a smile and slowly, with Anna's arm round her shoulders, Sharon Bell walked forward into their home.

Jane Carrick is the Pseudonym
of Mary Cummins
who also writes as
Mary Jane Warmington